五位小小美少女

FIRST EDITION 2011

Copyright © 2011 by

Talltale Underground Book Co. UnLtd.

ISBN 978-0-9807757-0-9

Calligraphy by Zhang Yun

NOTE: The abbreviation BCE (Before the Common Era)

used in this book is equivalent to BC

China — 96 BCE

In her disguise Lan Zhu-Ku stalks Emperor Ji Tuo. At a crowded market one morning the Emperor accidentally knocks a lady. He doesn't recognise the disguised woman is his former wife. He is very apologetic but she laughs him off. After they talk together happily for a moment the woman invites him to her home later in the week.

Days later Emperor Ji Tuo is found with his head sliced off. He will never seduce again.

From her hideout in the mountains Lan Zhu-Ku watches the panic. She seems delighted with herself, but her eyes remain determined.

There is more to be done, she thinks to herself while cleaning her sickle.

B. D. WHITE

CIRCUMSTANCES THAT SURROUND MR QUAH
FIVE LITTLE MAIDS

PART ONE

Chapter One

Japan — Today

"**W**hy don't you take a few weeks off work? Go for a nice holiday. Forget about the trial. Forget about this whole case."

Mr Quah directs his eyes up to the senior superintendent who is in charge of the local police headquarters where Mr Quah is a police officer. The superintendent looks down at Mr Quah hoping he will take the advice.

"Maybe," Mr Quah replies without emotion, continuing with his paperwork.

He has spent a difficult couple of months working with the prosecution of a violent robbery case. Events had not worked out how he intended. Throughout the lengthy court trial key witnesses suddenly changed their stories. Mr Quah suspected they were paid off by the defendant's associates. Mr Quah struggled to produce more compelling evidence against the accused until a previously unknown victim surfaced. Several investigators verified the victim's statement and this was enough for the three judges to sentence the accused to jail. The case was over and the prosecution had the verdict they wanted but Mr Quah was disappointed in himself. He wanted to be the best police officer he could be and he had let himself down.

"A holiday sounds like a good idea," Mr Quah says to his superintendent, but he is still not convinced.

Sophie has arranged to meet her new friend Kayami by the river. It is early morning. Very early. The sky is bright enough for Sophie to be able to see but the sun hasn't yet risen over the distant mountains.

"There she is," Kayami calls out.

Sophie sees her new friend Kayami stretching by the railing. Early as the day is, the path along the water has a large scattering of dedicated people all there to greet the morning sun.

Kayami is standing with three other women who Sophie assumes are Kayami's friends. All are doing various stretches and Tai Chi movements.

Sophie approaches Kayami feeling lively, ready for this new experience.

"Good morning," she says to Kayami.

Sophie observes the other three women, wondering how she is going to manage.

Kayami notices Sophie is apprehensive, fully aware that Sophie has never done Tai Chi before.

"Just copy us," Kayami says with an encouraging smile.

Kayami continues with her stretching movements. As Sophie begins copying Kayami she feels very awkward, like all eyes are watching her, but everyone else is focused on themselves. This crowd comes here every morning to empty their brains of thoughts and empty their bodies of stress.

"I feel strange," Sophie says to Kayami, "but I guess all these people along the river are doing the same as me so I should not be embarrassed."

Except that they have been doing Tai Chi for years, Sophie thinks to herself.

"Follow us slowly, there are no set rules. All you need to do is think of nothing," Kayami tells Sophie, and they both carry on.

After a few minutes Sophie is more comfortable. As she stretches and moves she focuses her ears on the birds that are waking up. She gazes out over the water and to the city on the other side of the river and watches the buildings turn orange as the sun rises. She can hear the street noise start to get louder as the city wakes up. Boats putter around beginning their daily routines.

Towards the end Sophie forgets she's doing Tai Chi until her group stops for the day.

"I really enjoyed that," she tells Kayami.

"We start every morning like this," one of Kayami's friends says to Sophie as she walks closer.

Sophie had not noticed until now that she is an elderly frail lady, but she appears very healthy. She introduces herself and the remaining two women to Sophie.

"I'm Miss Serizawa. This is Azuna and Fusako."

Both say hello by dipping their heads politely.

"Nice to meet you," Sophie says to all three while dipping her head in return.

Sophie introduces herself.

Azuna and Fusako appear to be the same age as Kayami and herself.

Sophie thinks that Miss Serizawa appears to be quite old, but something about her impresses Sophie. There is a sparkle in Miss Serizawa's eyes.

Whatever she is doing is working, Sophie thinks.

She hopes she'll look half as good in her later years.

Before departing ways, the five agree to meet there again the next morning.

Sophie looks down at an address on a scrap of newspaper that she had cut out of the employment section of the morning's paper during breakfast.

'38d,' she reads to herself.

The house numbering system is difficult for Sophie to work out.

She finally stops walking and glances up at building number 38. After a deep breath she walks to the front archway of unit d, located on the ground floor.

Barely over the threshold of the archway, Sophie is startled by a loud voice.

"Yes, hello!"

The voice sounds very impatient.

As Sophie's eyes adjust she sees a man sitting at a messy desk, hunched over his work.

"I'm here about the cleaning job," she explains, holding out the scrap of newspaper as proof.

"You do clean before?" the man asks.

He fails to make eye contact with Sophie. The loudness of his voice is maintained, indicating he talks loudly in general conversation, which Sophie finds is a bit unsettling.

"Well yes, I've cleaned before," Sophie says nervously.

She is beginning to wish she had not bothered coming.

"Ah yes, very good. You start in morning. What size shirt you are?" the man asks.

With pen poised he gets ready to write the information down in his files, which Sophie notices is an old piece of paper with writing and numbers all over it already.

Sophie gives her shirt size to the crazy man and in return she gets the address of the apartment building she will be cleaning.

"You need ride there?" he offers, finally looking up from his work.

Sophie hesitates for a minute.

"I guess that will be easier than a train or bus," she says.

"You meet here, 8 o'clock."

His eyes fall back to his desk.

"Yes, thank you," she says while walking out.

'What am I in for?'

"See you!" he calls out as she leaves.

Despite the thick smog in the air the residents of a mountain town go about their day as usual. Mist or fog can be bad enough but when pollution joins with water in the air visibility becomes almost non-existent. On days like this the locals know to ride their bicycles slower than on foggy days and they also know to be extra careful before they walk across the roads.

A woman walking along one of the lanes is enjoying her time in the smog. She likes having a small circle of visible space around her. The smog is like a curtain which she can hide behind. Occasionally an oncoming pedestrian's visible circle mixes with hers but that doesn't last long. There is hardly enough time to acknowledge the person before they disappear. She finds her way to a traffic island in the centre of town where she meets two friends.

The three women have arranged to meet in the centre of town at midday. They have been informed that a member of the community uses his high-ranking status as the biggest employer in the region to take advantage of his female employees. Here he comes now, as he does every day, walking to his favourite restaurant for lunch.

The three women let a bus go past, they smile at a cyclist who rides by, they pin the businessman's arms behind his back and they snap his neck before finally separating to disappear behind the smog curtain. He is still twitching as a taxi slams on the brakes, coming to a stop millimetres from the body. The area begins to fill with onlookers.

Mr Quah has decided to take the advice of his superintendent. He was right in suggesting Mr Quah go away for a while. A seat on the afternoon train south is booked and paid for. Mr Quah is currently packing his suitcase in his apartment on the twenty-third floor in which he lives fifty weeks of the year.

'A break sounds very nice. Change is always good. Thoughts will be put to rest,' he keeps telling himself.

Mr Quah sighs as his eyes wander around his room. After a pause he is satisfied he has everything he needs.

He closes his suitcase up and leaves his apartment for the elevator.

In the course of the taxi ride to the train station Mr Quah wonders what he will do for fourteen days.

Before boarding his train Mr Quah buys some food to eat during his journey.

"Oh, and I'll also buy the evening newspaper," he tells the shop assistant when he pays for the food.

With the train speeding along Mr Quah reads the newspaper while he eats. Actually he only glances at the newspaper pages. He has never been very interested in them and mainly bought the paper for something to do in between napping and watching the scenery fly by at mind-boggling speeds. A headline catches his weary eyes and Mr Quah has to look twice: '*In the fog.*'

Perhaps he is reminded of a story written in 1901 of the same name that he recalls reading many moons ago when he couldn't put down old detective stories, so he reads the article:

'A body was found today by a taxi driver in the middle of a busy street full of witnesses who saw nothing due to the thick smog that engulfed the area. The police first thought the taxi had hit the well-known local businessman but the injuries do not support this allegation. They now fear the death may be caused by something more sinister. Mr Higashi leaves behind his loving wife and four children.'

Now where have I heard that name before? Mr Higashi sounds very familiar.

This is going to bug him the entire time he is meant to be resting.

Why am I on this train?

Mr Quah knew holidaying would be a mistake. He wishes he were back in the city where he can access files and reports.

For the rest of the journey Mr Quah searches under the couch, in the drawers and cupboards, on the shelves and under the bed in his brain, trying to remember why the name stands out.

Mr Quah barely notices changing trains in Fukuoka. He has to keep his mind on the task at hand.

When he finally alights from the train carriage Mr Quah quickly carries his suitcase to a taxi and they set off on the final leg of his journey.

Home at last. Mr Quah's taxi stops along an esplanade. This is where he comes to escape the city. If he can ever tear away from the city's strong arms he would move here permanently.

Mr Quah hops out and takes a long breath of the sea air. As the taxi drives away Mr Quah turns and scans his house and front yard while he crosses the road. He knows what had to happen for him to afford this house but he catches his thoughts before the pain hits too deep.

The closest library will be shut by now so Mr Quah must wait until morning before he can search through newspapers and computer files for information on the businessman named Higashi. It will be a long wait.

He decides to unpack his suitcase and go for a walk into town.

Moments later all the windows are ajar to allow fresh air inside his home. With the chest of drawers in his bedroom now full of clothes, Mr Quah is ready to go for a walk.

While Mr Quah strolls along the neighbouring lanes he immediately notices that this little town has not changed a bit since he was here last. It never will. The residents of this small fishing town do exactly what their ancestors have done all through time. Half an hour later, Mr Quah stops at a shop where he buys necessary supplies. On his walk home he buys hot food from a street vendor. He sits and eats the grilled fish right then and there while the sun sinks down over the bay. Children run around laughing. Not a car in sight. He almost relaxes there for a minute.

The next morning Sophie meets her new friends by the river for Tai Chi.

"Good morning Miss Serizawa. Hello Azuna, Fusako and Kayami," Sophie says as she bows to each.

"You got all our names right," Miss Serizawa says.

They begin their Tai Chi movements right away while many others along the river are also commencing their morning exercises. Sophie still feels a bit uncomfortable with other people around but she finds she enjoys the stretching more today.

"I am slowly getting used to the moves," she tells Azuna who is standing on her left.

"Give the routine a few weeks," Azuna replies.

"So long as you relax the Tai Chi is working," Fusako tells Sophie.

After Tai Chi the five bid each other good day.

Sophie strides home with a new spring in her step.

"How did you go today?" Alana asks.

Sophie is preparing lunch for her daughter.

"Better. Not totally comfortable."

"It's only your second time. Mastering the moves probably takes years," Alana says.

"I hope not."

Moments later Sophie walks her daughter to school and then, wondering if she is heading for her doom, catches a bus to the crazy man's unit. To her surprise this actually seems like a decent little business he has going. Half a dozen people are standing by a van. She joins them and the man from yesterday's job interview comes out of the place. Sophie assumes he is the owner of the business.

"I have shirt for you," he says to Sophie, handing her a plastic wrapped green shirt.

The others are already wearing their green shirts. Sophie realises the shirts have a cartoon version of the man on the breast pocket with the slogan, *'we the best to clean you mess.'*

Sophie receives directions to the toilets from the owner and hurries inside to change into her green work shirt.

Before long Sophie is in the back of the van, with the other employees, heading to her new job. She is happy to be working but she is nervous.

I hope the work will not be too strenuous, Sophie thinks to herself.

"Don't look at me like that."

Mr Quah is standing in his garage early the next morning. His car sits innocently, gazing up into his eyes. Man's second best friend. Mr Quah never needs to drive in the city. He loves coming home and having the car there waiting. The car misses him just as much. It needs to stretch its legs.

Moments later the engine hums along the coastal road, breathing the fresh morning air into its lungs. Mr Quah can't stop grinning. Nothing much makes him grin like this.

Mr Quah spends the morning at the public library. He had no problem finding the name Mr Higashi due to the fact that he was a successful businessman from a very early age. Mr Quah has had to filter through all of these articles. He finally reads an old newspaper report hidden away from the top stories of the day. Mr Higashi's wife allegedly attacked him one night many years ago. Police were called. No charges were laid.

The report in the newspaper is very brief. This information may not be connected in any way to the unfortunate death of the man but Mr Quah decides to pursue this. He makes a phone call.

Half an hour later Mr Quah hangs up the pay phone and walks out of the public library a little wiser. He had made two calls. One was to the police station situated in the town where Mr Higashi lived and worked. That phone call was pointless. The police there would not say one word about any alleged attack carried out by an angry wife. Mr Quah then went to the source.

He called the local newspaper which had printed the brief story years earlier.

The supervisor says, "One hour after the words were on sale for the public to read, Mr Higashi went to the courts and was successful in having any further damaging articles about him stopped. The incident was never to be thought about in future."

Mr Quah thanks the man for his time. He drives home with one thought on his mind: Surely this was a revenge attack, but why now?

Mr Quah arrives home and packs his bags. He prepares himself for the journey back to civilization. Back to his suffocating apartment. He has work to do. His holiday can wait.

The first few hours of Sophie's new cleaning job fly by. She actually enjoys the work because each cleaner is allocated a floor, comprising eight apartments, and they are left alone to dust, vacuum, wash floors and clean the bathrooms. It's lunchtime before she knows it.

Sophie goes for a walk down the street and soon comes to a small corner shop. She enters, buys her lunch and takes her food outside to eat. Another cleaner comes along with their lunch and sits with Sophie and they start talking.

"Are you a student?" the young woman asks Sophie.

"No, I've just moved here with my daughter. Cleaning is easy work for now. I'll find something more full-time eventually. What about you?"

"I am studying at night to be a nurse," the young woman tells Sophie.

"That's excellent. You have also studied English at some stage."

The young woman goes shy.

"Most school students are learning to speak English now, but I am not very good at reading English," she says.

"Learning a new language is very hard. I am having trouble with my Japanese but everything takes time," Sophie says.

After lunch Sophie continues cleaning the rooms ₁ and at three o'clock the employees all meet by the van to head back to their side of town.

"We need to," Alana tells her mum as they sit at the dining table that evening.

"I guess."

Sophie knows nothing about cars. She feels she doesn't really need one. Her employer drives her and her work mates to jobs but she has to catch buses or trams to the shopping centres and everywhere else they decide to go.

She turns to her daughter.

"I admit I should buy a car, or at least start looking. Owning a car will make life easier."

Alana asks, "Until then can we hire one? Hire a small car for a few days per week."

Alana really wants her mum to buy a car so life is more convenient for them both.

"Alright, I'll think about hiring a car. In the meantime how about we visit some car yards to see what's out there?"

"That sounds great," Alana says.

She is happy. No more walking to school or catching the bus to her sporting events.

Chapter Two

Every morning for the rest of the week Sophie meets her friends by the river and wouldn't have things any other way. Although this means waking earlier than she likes, Sophie loves watching the city come to life. Three days that week she cleans apartments. Time drags on a little while cleaning and the job can be physically challenging at times but all in all she is very happy with her new life.

On Thursday afternoon Sophie is walking her daughter Alana home from school. Alana mentions that Rieko, Kayami's daughter, has invited them both to go shopping on Saturday morning.

"There is a little shopping district about twenty minutes away by tram. Rieko has told me that there are narrow streets all leading off each other and you get lost in the maze of shops," Alana tells her mum.

Alana fell in love with the idea and couldn't wait to tell her mum who likes the idea just as much.

"Travelling out to a shopping district will be great fun," Sophie says.

Sophie imagines tiny streets and small market shops selling all kinds of items.

"Expanding my friendship with Kayami will also be nice," she tells her daughter.

At the next morning's Tai Chi session Sophie tells Kayami she will be there on Saturday.

"Both Alana and myself are looking forward to going with you and Rieko."

"Near the tram stop is a park with an old fountain. We'll meet you there," Kayami explains.

The weather is perfect as Sophie and Alana walk from their house to the tram stop Saturday morning. Both are excited about going to the shopping district with their new friends. Alana mainly wants to shop for clothes and Sophie really wants to find pieces of old furniture. After hopping off the tram, the two walk to a park situated across the road where they can see the fountain.

Kayami and Rieko are sitting there waiting patiently.

"Good morning," Sophie says to Kayami.

"There are lots of shops around the streets, let's get going!" Rieko says excitedly.

The daughters agree to meet their mothers back at the fountain for lunch and run off. Sophie and Kayami walk around together and discover shops are filled with clothes, home wares, flowers, antiques and books. Sophie even wanders into a shop full of robotic toys and shelves of electronic gadgets that she has never heard of before.

Sophie has never been to such a place as this shopping district and she is very pleased at having been invited. She loves the narrow side streets where she discovers many smaller shops. She wants to find a nice antique wood cabinet but doesn't see any. One shop that they come across contains rare old books. Sophie spends a few moments in there browsing the shelves. Some of the books are behind glass and appear too fragile to touch. Although they look very interesting, she knows nothing about books so she doesn't stay in the shop for very long. She meets Kayami out on the street and they continue going from shop to shop. Many people are shopping now, due to the nice weather, and many bargains have been found, as evidenced by the fact that most of the shoppers who walk along hold bags under their arms. The vibe is exciting.

Sophie feels odd at one point though. For a brief moment she feels like she is being followed.

Probably just me worrying about nothing as usual.

Sophie scans the faces of the happy shoppers but doesn't see anything suspicious so she ignores her fears and goes back to shopping.

Within the next hour Sophie has bought a new wok, some casual tops and an old vase.

Then she finally comes across a furniture store full of traditional styled pieces. Sophie rushes in and sees they have a nice old carved wood cabinet for sale.

"How much will you sell this for?"

The shopkeeper tells Sophie how much he is asking.

Sophie has a second look at the old cabinet. She isn't sure about the price but she can't resist.

"We deliver for you."

With this news the shopkeeper wins her over. Sophie pays for the cabinet and gives her address to the shopkeeper.

"I think I am all shopped out," Sophie tells Kayami once they are outside the store.

"I agree completely," Kayami replies.

They carry their goods through the labyrinth of laneways until Kayami spots the park with the fountain.

Sophie is so happy with her purchases as Kayami walks with her to the fountain. They sit and talk while waiting for their daughters to meet them.

"Have you found a job yet?" Kayami asks.

"I've found a cleaning job. Cleaning apartments. The headquarters is ten minutes bus ride away from my house. We all pile into the owners van and he drops us off. I'm happy with that until I buy a car and drive," Sophie says.

Kayami asks, "How are you finding the work?"

"Cleaning is easy enough. The owner is crazy. Mr Nguyen. I think he is Vietnamese," Sophie says.

Sophie realises she doesn't know what Kayami does for a living.

"Where do you work?"

"Miss Serizawa owns a restaurant, that's where we all met, so I work there nearly thirty hours a week. I have been working there eight years. She is actually looking for some help. The restaurant is only open in the evenings, six days a week. I could put in a good word for you if you'd like to be a waitress or help in the kitchen," offers Kayami.

"Yes, thank you, I'd like that," Sophie says.

She will love to work a few hours there every other night.

Alana and Rieko eventually struggle over with their full shopping bags.

Alana exclaims, "I bought tops and pants and a dress."

"I bought a bag of crystals and clothes as well," Rieko says.

Alana has even found a thirty centimetre oval mirror for the dressing table in her bedroom.

"My old mirror was damaged when we moved," she explains.

They carry their piles of shopping to the tram stop. Kayami and Rieko say goodbye and walk off to their car while Sophie and Alana catch the tram home. As Sophie had hoped, the outing with their new friends was very enjoyable.

"Mum, this is excellent!"

To Alana's delight, Sophie has finally succumbed to driving. She has rented a car and surprised her daughter.

"I know. Sorry I didn't organise a car sooner. Now I can go alone to clean houses that Mr Nguyen books for me, rather than be bussed in with fellow employees cleaning apartments all day."

"I thought you were just going for a walk around the block. What made you want a car today?" Alana asks.

"Kayami mentioned she might be able to talk to her friend and find me some work. You know, I've mentioned Miss Serizawa to you. She owns a restaurant. So I have taken a gamble and rented a car for us."

This allows Sophie to have more freedom as well as give her ever-changing scenery.

"You won't regret it."

She has not officially told Alana yet, but Sophie is seriously considering buying a car when more money flows in.

Monday night, Sophie and Alana have been invited to try the food at Miss Serizawa's restaurant. This is an opportunity for Sophie and Alana to see what the place is like. Sophie and Alana park their hire car around the corner from Miss Serizawa's restaurant.

Outside the façade is an old three-storey building with a traditional Japanese tiled roof, nestled between two tall skyscrapers. Inside the place is packed with customers all eating the much talked about food.

"Look, Mum," Alana says, pointing to a massive lobster tank.

After a moment of lining up, Sophie and Alana are shown to their table.

Once seated, the waiter hands them each a menu. Sophie glances around the packed restaurant. Most of the patrons are families. All are talking loudly within their groups, animated so they can be understood and heard over others seated near them.

Alana has been watching the activity in the kitchen. There are cutouts in the wall so that customers can see through to watch their meals being cooked.

"I can't see how they all know what to do. Organised chaos," Alana says.

Sophie spots Azuna and gives a small wave.

"If every night is like this I am sure the chefs and waiters must be used to how busy the kitchen becomes by now. Each person would have a specific task," Sophie explains.

The waiter approaches and Sophie and Alana order their meals.

"What do you think of the place, Mum?" Alana asks.

"Apart from being so busy? Miss Serizawa has done a good job. Look at the line now. It's almost out the door."

Moments later they are eating the delicious food. The table is covered in plates and bowls with a wide variety of different foods to sample.

"Wow, there is so much flavour. Are you handling the spice alright?" Alana asks.

Sophie's eyes are watering. She has another sip of water.

"I might leave the rest of that plate and finish the other food," Sophie says.

"It's all so dainty."

After Sophie and Alana have eaten their main courses, neither can fit in dessert, Miss Serizawa comes over to say hello and talk with them.

"Kayami has told me you are looking for work. I need floor staff and kitchen staff. If you would like to do either please let me know. Do you have experience?" Miss Serizawa asks.

"I have been a waitress, years ago. I do cook at home all the time but I doubt that my food is restaurant quality, but I could always help wash dishes or clean up after the chefs," Sophie says.

Miss Serizawa has a suggestion.

"Come here Wednesday night and you can wait tables. How does that sound?"

"Perfect, I'll be here," Sophie says, very pleased.

Not long later, after Sophie catches sight of Kayami and waves, Sophie and Alana head home. Things couldn't be better. Everything is going great in this new world they've entered.

Venice — 1541

A person hurries along the canals early one morning. They have arranged to travel on a trading vessel and their wooden trunk was carted off the previous evening. They are very eager to be reunited with their possessions. The sun will be up in an hour and they hope to be well out to sea by then. This person knows the laneways and canals perfectly.

Turn left and walk over the small bridge. Turn right and cross the piazza.

Empty now, the space will soon be full of merchants and townspeople. At the next bridge they stop and listen back. Predictably they can hear faint footsteps echoing through the piazza. The person is being followed and begins walking again, taking a small sickle from a waist sling. At an archway up ahead the person hides in the shadows and waits silently for the distant footsteps of the pursuer to grow louder and louder on the stone path. In the shadows the pursued holds their breath as they wait for the perfect moment to show off their ancient knife fighting skills.

Shocked by the ambush, barely a gasp is expelled by the pursuer as he clutches at his heart and collapses to the cold ground. The culprit is ten strides away by this time. They turn right and climb down stone steps into an empty Gondola. Nobody is around to miss it. Rowing across the water the person is worried about being out in the open, but they make the short journey across to the other side of the Grand Canal without being spotted.

Safely at the other side of the canal the person washes their sickle in the water and makes their way on foot to the Venice Port. They walk alongside the merchant ships until they see the one that will take them far away from here.

They approach the boat in time to see the last of the goods being loaded. The person has to assume their possessions are safe down in the cargo hold.

"Signora," a soldier calls to her.

The soldier walks up to our murderer and notices the woman is from the Orient. Being the busiest port in the world he does not think twice about this minor detail. He tries to talk with her but the language barrier makes attempting this difficult.

The soldier notices she is keeping her eyes on a couple of trunks being loaded on to the boat. He assumes she is a merchant like everyone else and wishes her a safe journey.

She walks up the ramp and lets out a deep breath.

This boat will take her down the Adriatic Sea to freedom. The woman is excited at the thought of where she may end up next. Off they sail.

Chapter Three

"**M**iss Serizawa has owned the restaurant for thirty-two years. Over that period of time the restaurant has grown in reputation. Very popular with locals but many others travel great lengths to eat here."

A kitchen-hand is talking to Sophie one evening during a break from working.

"I notice the line of patrons stretches out the door nearly every night," Sophie says.

"Her food is the subject of many magazine and newspaper reviews all over Japan, not to mention praise every night by the patrons."

Occasionally there are quiet moments in the restaurant and Sophie uses these opportunities to talk with either Miss Serizawa, Azuna, Fusako or Kayami. Sophie learns they are all very interesting and unique people.

Sophie has pieced together that Miss Serizawa and Azuna met about fifteen years ago. Azuna came into the restaurant one day and offered to be partners. Miss Serizawa said no, but added that Azuna could work there if she really liked the place.

"I accepted and have been working here ever since. Miss Serizawa opened the restaurant from boredom really. She was tired of cooking for just herself," Azuna tells Sophie.

Miss Serizawa designed the look of the interior and employed a group of a dozen staff that made the restaurant a nice homely place to eat. When Azuna started there she told her friends to come. One was a magazine editor who gave Miss Serizawa rave reviews.

"I read a review and applied at the restaurant to be a chef," Fusako says.

Miss Serizawa and Azuna loved Fusako's cooking and the three worked together, very hard, as the customers lined up outside the front door. Patrons had to book a table many weeks in advance. Miss Serizawa was forced to buy the two floors above the restaurant to cope with the amount of customers. Later Kayami was hired as a waitress and has been there eight years now. Sophie is keen to prove she can be a valued employee.

Tuesday morning, after Sophie had done Tai Chi with her friends, Miss Serizawa invites Sophie to her house. Once or twice a week the four meet to talk about work. They usually just end up bickering about the world. Sophie says she will love to visit Miss Serizawa's home and thanks her for the invitation.

"Come over at midday," Miss Serizawa says and gives Sophie directions to her house.

"I'll see you there," Sophie says happily as she walks to her hire car.

At quarter to one, Sophie drives slowly along a narrow street. She has finished cleaning for the morning and is on her way to Miss Serizawa's house. Sophie will be late but Miss Serizawa knows Sophie had to clean this morning.

She has not been to this neighbourhood before but Sophie has faith she won't get lost because she is not far from Miss Serizawa's restaurant so she doesn't panic too much. She pulls her car over to the side of the road, stopping to check her map one last time. A car drives past that

Sophie recognizes for some reason. She is sure she has seen the car a few times lately. Maybe they're lost too.

She laughs at herself for even noticing it. The map says to turn right so she obeys.

Further up this road on the right is a house being built. Sophie pulls over and talks to one of the builders.

"Excuse me. I'm looking for number four."

The builder says, "I think four must be further down there a bit more."

He points to a driveway covered in trees.

"Thank you," Sophie says and drives on a little way until she finally finds Miss Serizawa's house.

Sophie is impressed. The streets are narrow here and all the houses seem crammed in together, but as she parks and walks into Miss Serizawa's grounds Sophie feels like she is out in the countryside somewhere. Miss Serizawa must have the biggest block of land for miles around. Massive trees shield the house from the outside world. This house must have been in Miss Serizawa's family for many years. Normally buying land of this size in a city would be impossible.

There are expensive cars parked along the side of the house. Sophie recognises one is Kayami's. She feels excited as she approaches the front door. The house is huge. The architecture is clearly of an older style but some renovations and additional rooms built on during the 1970's give the house a modern feel.

Miss Serizawa must have been trendy, Sophie thinks as she knocks at the door.

Azuna answers shortly after.

"Hello Azuna," Sophie says, delighted to be welcomed inside such a house.

"Come through," Azuna says and waves Sophie into the entry hall, which is nearly bigger than her house.

Sophie follows Azuna through a wide hallway. They pass closed doors until they arrive at a large rear room which overlooks the garden at the back of Miss Serizawa's house. Miss Serizawa, Fusako and Kayami are all sitting on couches. They smile as Sophie comes into the room. Azuna shows Sophie a seat on one of the four plush

leather couches that face each other in the
centre of the room.

"How are you?" Kayami asks as she
pours Sophie a wine.

"Great thank you," Sophie says, taking
the glass.

"Welcome to my home," Miss Serizawa
says.

"Oh, it's so lovely," Sophie says,
surveying the huge lounge room,
wondering where all the doors may lead.

"Did you find us okay?" Fusako
asks while taking a tray of food from a
maid.

"The house numbering system is
different from where I used to live so
apart from consulting my map a few
times, I was fine," Sophie chuckles.

"How are you coping at the restaurant,
Sophie?" Azuna asks while she sips her
drink.

"The work is enjoyable," Sophie says,
"and fast paced. Very busy and loud
in there, but I like keeping busy and
remembering who orders what meals.
The time passes by really quickly."

The topic turns to children.

"They're a handful but if they ever move out I'll miss them," Azuna says.

She looks at Sophie and Kayami and adds, "You two still have a few more years with yours."

"Yes, but our children are not at the rebellious stage yet so things are fine at the moment," Kayami says.

The topic turns to husbands. Sophie doesn't feel comfortable to tell them too much about her past so she is keeping quiet. As she gets to know them she'll talk about herself more.

Fusako says, "They're a handful. I'm joking. My husband works all week. I miss him so much and love the weekends with him. And we get to go away for a few weeks every year."

Sophie is enjoying listening to the women talk but she notices Miss Serizawa is quiet too.

The women talk more while enjoying fine food and finer wine. Sophie wonders how long they are planning to sit there. She is not used to this and can't relax. She eventually makes her excuses and leaves.

"I am not used to this life," Sophie tells Kayami on the front porch.

"You will become adjusted over time. I understand how you feel—new friends and a new way of life. It took me a while to get used to having these women in my life," Kayami says, making Sophie feel better.

"See you at work," Sophie says.

She walks past the shiny silver expensive vehicles to her old rental car.

From conversing with both the staff and the patrons at the restaurant Sophie finds out why Miss Serizawa doesn't talk about herself much. It turns out Miss Serizawa has never married.

"She likes to keep to herself," one customer tells her.

Sophie feels a bit sorry for Miss Serizawa. Most people do. But Miss Serizawa is happy.

"The restaurant keeps her motivated," another customer adds.

Sophie has to remember that some patrons have probably been eating here since the restaurant opened and would consider Miss Serizawa a friend.

At home Miss Serizawa reads many books and no one would believe that she actually enjoys watching television, keeping up to date with the latest news and treads. Television wasn't around when Miss Serizawa was young. Nothing much was around back then, but that allowed for few distractions. All that her and her friends could do when not studying was to make their own fun. She wonders how young people of today cope with so many distractions.

Miss Serizawa doesn't have any pets. She did when growing up with her family. By the time she was middle aged Miss Serizawa couldn't deal with the loss anymore. You buy your pet, love and nurture the new addition to the family until the animal dies. You rush out and replace the dead creature with a new pet, briefly filling a void, only for events to happen all over again. This doesn't seem right to her. No, she enjoys being alone with her thoughts. Some people might not, but she's used to a life full of solitude by now. She can believe what she thinks and trusts her thoughts. She wakes up happy, does her Tai Chi every morning, tidies the house and garden, has a light lunch, sits and reads nearly every day and then walks to her restaurant in the afternoon to prepare for the crowds that flock there at night. She is quite content.

"Taxi drivers sleep in little designated rooms in city buildings, not going home until the weekend, as the distance is too far to travel morning and night every day," a kitchen-hand tells Sophie.

Sophie has just learnt that to not go home all week is common practise for people who work in big cities in Japan.

"Not the life for me," Sophie says.

The families of workers in the cities become adjusted and even grow proud of the worker because they know how hard the world is out there.

Azuna and Fusako's husbands work in a big city. Not as taxi drivers. Both work in separate buildings moving money around. They eat at the restaurant every couple of weeks but to their knowledge neither has met the other and probably don't know their wives are friends. On the weekends they catch the bullet train hundreds of kilometres home to their loving wives and get to see their children. Time is flying by. Their children are almost all in their late teens now.

Occasionally each of the husbands wonders, 'why work so hard until retirement?'

Life is full of isolation. Is missing their children turning into adults and not spending time with their loving wives worth the stress?

As soon as the husbands see home however they see why. Their houses are huge. Each has luxurious holidays every year with their families. Both own expensive cars and furniture. To the highly successful members of society the effort in working hard for a better life is worth a few sacrifices.

Singapore — 1826

Night begins to drape itself gently over the town, while a child watches the community scrambling to pack up their goods and race home. When ants are threatened they double their speed without a second thought. The ants know that lives are at stake. Every night the citizens of this town behave in a similar fashion to the scared ants. With darkness comes death. The inhabitants believe a shadow will randomly snatch a life for no apparent reason because this has been happening almost weekly for quite some time now.

The child, however, is not scared. The young soul has noticed a pattern and believes this is not random.

While people almost knock the child over to hurry home, the child is quite calm.

If you have not done anything to harm people or objects around you, the child believes, you avoid coming under the spell of justice.

When the sky becomes black the child is almost home and sees two shadows in the distance. One is seemingly feminine. The two shadows enter a dwelling. The child waits. Not long later the feminine shadow exits and disappears. Tonight's victim has met with the Annihilator of all man. The child walks safely home, correct in believing they were never in any danger.

Chapter Four

Sophie has needed to buy a car for weeks now. She decides that today is the day. Her friends all have expensive cars so she feels left out showing up in her rental.

"I won't be able to afford anything like Kayami has but I've been working for a while, I don't mind digging into my savings," Sophie tells her daughter who is very pleased.

She only wants a small car, nothing too fancy. So long as the car looks nice. The hire car is too costly. Not to mention embarrassing.

"I can't wait," Alana says.

After getting ready, Sophie and Alana catch a bus to the city.

They stay away from new car lots. Sophie wants an economical second hand car.

Alana spots a dealership across the road.

"Used cars there, Mum," Alana points.

Sophie doesn't know much about car brands. She just wants a car that is in nice condition, with no visible rust or dents and drives smoothly.

They hop off the bus and walk over to the car yard.

She sees a little two-door hatch just as a sales man approaches.

"This will get you from A to B. Slowly. This car has had one owner, an old man who went from his house to the shops and back once a week. The car would suit someone like him," the man informs Sophie.

"Well I won't be driving much. Just to and from work each day," Sophie tells him.

"Sounds like you need something a bit bigger. We have had some cars come in recently, follow me over here."

He urges Sophie to go and look at bigger, more expensive cars.

Sophie doesn't budge and says, "No, I'm happy with this little run around. There are no dents and I'm sure the old man had the engine serviced regularly."

But the salesman wants Sophie to consider the other cars.

"Goodbye."

Sophie walks off with Alana close behind. They both agree he was too pushy. Sophie is turned off from buying a car today.

That afternoon Sophie drives to Miss Serizawa's house. Sophie turns into Miss Serizawa's driveway, completely unaware that the car, which has been following her for a few days now, pulls over further down the road. Sophie walks to Miss Serizawa's front door and is let inside.

For reasons Sophie doesn't yet fully understand, a habit is developing in that their meetings are beginning to turn into bicker sessions. The five air their annoyances of the world. To anyone observing the conversations, the women seem harmless enough. They are quite calm about what they say and usually have a few laughs. And a few glasses of wine.

Today's meeting begins with the five friends sitting in the spacious lounge room talking about make-up.

"I don't like to use much make-up," Sophie says.

"Have you ever had your make-up done for you?" Azuna asks.

"No, never," Sophie replies.

"We could do your make-up for you. Miss Serizawa has a lot of products. She was previously involved in the theatre," Fusako says.

"Oh, okay," Sophie says with hesitation, not liking the idea of these people touching her face.

"Come on," Miss Serizawa says, "don't be shy. I've done make-up for many stars when I was younger. You'll like the results."

They all walk to the bathroom down the hall.

"This will be fun," Kayami says to Sophie.

"We'll do your make-up next," Azuna says to Kayami.

The bathroom is three times bigger than Sophie's- easily accommodating the five of them. Fusako, Azuna and Kayami watch on while Miss Serizawa applies Sophie's make-up.

To start with Miss Serizawa only does the eye liner and foundation. To Sophie's surprise the results looks good. She feels pampered.

Kayami now has her turn so she hops into the chair.

"I feel like a movie star," Kayami says when the make-up has been applied.

"How long have you been involved in the theatre, Miss Serizawa?" Sophie asks.

"Oh, a number of years back in my college days. I helped out here and there. Seems like forever ago now," Miss Serizawa says.

Sophie and Kayami feel more comfortable now and are sure that is all for today. They are wrong.

"Sit in the chair again Sophie," Miss Serizawa says.

Sophie does, wondering why.

"Close your eyes."

When Sophie opens her eyes she doesn't realise she is looking at her reflection in the mirror. Staring back at her is a pure white skinned oriental woman.

"What happened?" Sophie asks, a bit shocked and not knowing quite what to think of her new face.

"This is the Maiko look. I can teach you how to do this for yourself at home," Miss Serizawa says.

Sophie wonders, 'Why would I want to look like this?'

"There are even costumes here," Azuna says.

Fusako opens a cupboard.

Sophie is shocked. They must be from old plays.

Kayami sits back in the chair, ready for her face to be transformed. Miss Serizawa gets to work.

Kayami loves the attention and appears quite happy after the application of make-up has been completed.

Why not play dress ups, Sophie tries telling herself, although she considers the activity very odd.

Sophie decides to mention that she went to buy a car from a car yard earlier in the day.

"He wouldn't listen to me. I liked the little car. He didn't care. All he wanted to do was show me more expensive ones," she tells them.

"We shouldn't have to put up with that type of thing," Azuna says.

"I've been in that kind of situation before," Fusako adds.

"We can't change the world but we can change the minds of the people we deal with. Teach them a lesson or two in customer relations," Miss Serizawa laughs.

Sophie nods.

By the time Sophie removes her make-up, tidies up the bathroom and begins to leave Miss Serizawa's house Sophie reflects on the events that have happened. Overall Sophie's time with her new friends this afternoon has been very enjoyable.

Sophie is glad to have met Kayami. She is glad to have met all these women. She left her home as a widow with her daughter to move to a new world hoping to find happiness. Sophie is beginning to feel that, without forgetting her past, which she remembers fondly every day, she has found her new home. She feels she is going to like this place.

PART TWO

Chapter Five

"**H**ere's one!" Alana tells her mum as she reads the local newspaper.

"Read the ad," Sophie tries to act interested.

The thought of buying a car has not fully sunk in but Alana begins to read.

"Two door hatch-back. Only three years old. Hardly driven. Runs nicely."

Alana turns to face her mum.

"The ad sounds alright. Writing 'hardly driven' usually means the opposite," Sophie says and continues cooking breakfast.

Alana frowns.

"Mum! Don't be negative. Let's just have a look at the car and talk to the owner. This one is not from a car yard," she says.

"I'll ring them," Sophie says.

She is sceptical. She knows people lie.

An hour later, Sophie is test-driving the two-door hatchback.

The owner, a quiet spoken little man, is sitting next to her.

"I have the car serviced every few months," he explains, "I'm selling this because my wife doesn't drive much so we will share her car to save money."

Sophie likes the feel of the small car which is perfect for her, she admits to herself, as they drive back to the owner's home.

"How was the test drive?" Alana asks her mum.

She has been waiting on the street excitedly for her mum to come back.

"The car is very nice," Sophie quietly tells her daughter.

She knows she should have a mechanic go over the engine for her first to make sure the car is in good running order, but she doesn't know any mechanics. She trusts that the man has cared for the car. The paint is perfect. The driveway doesn't have any oil stains visible, which indicates there is no fluid leaking from the engine. Sophie talks with the owner.

"I do like the car. I will call in tomorrow with the money."

"Excellent. Thank you. Have a good day," he tells them.

Each time she does her make-up Kayami is finding the process easier. All she needs is lots of white paint. She enjoys applying the paint and foundation, seeing the transformation. After putting the oil on her eyebrows she begins styling her hair. Kayami goes slowly with her hair to get the correct style so this takes the longest amount of time. By the end she looks completely different. She gets excited each time she sees the results. The excitement is short lived though as she thinks about what she might be doing with her friends later in the night.

A child by the name of Tian should be in bed sleeping at this time of the night. Every night his mother tucks him into bed, and every night the boy waits for his mother to go to bed. He then gets up and plays with his toys, kneeling at his desk in the moon light, on the seventh floor of the apartment block. On one such night, as his favourite soldier destroys his least favourite monster, the boy looks out the window. An orange glow down on the street has caught his attention. He watches as a shop burns and four little white figures disappear, scattering off into the darkness.

The following morning a young man is driving to work. He wishes he had eaten a bigger breakfast. Stopped at a red light the young man has enough time for a little daydream. Just as he imagines delving into a nice hot lunch his senses re-awaken quite suddenly as a news report airs on the radio:

". . . *quite damaging. They seem to be random acts. We are hoping they don't become more violent. At this stage nobody has been seriously hurt. Half a dozen homes and shops have been destroyed. Witnesses have seen white shadowy figures disapp-earing into the night. People are wondering if they are ghosts taking their anger out on us. If anyone out there can help please call my office direct—Chief of the Metropolitan Police Department . . . ."*

The traffic lights turn green.

* * *

While at lunch a lady working as a journalist at a small newspaper company is being told by her boss, Mr Oshiro, what to write in her next article. Mr Oshiro wants to put a story in his newspaper about the 'four little maids', as the radio stations are calling them, which everyone is so scared of.

"No other newspaper is writing articles about these four women," she tells him.

"Exactly why we are going to," he answers back.

The newspapers have all silently agreed, made an unwritten rule, to not talk about these women and build up hype. The radio stations are working with the police to inform and warn the public about the four women but this newspaper boss wants part of the action.

"The population fears these women. Why keep the fear going? Why encourage the women and give them the exposure they want? Let us not make mention of them," she pleads.

"People out there want to know. They are hearing the radio reports and are all very interested, even if the news scares them out of their wits. The public constantly craves new things. We'll put a story in for tomorrow's paper and make a huge pile of money out of this," he says proudly.

He has made up his mind.

"You are just giving these women what they want," the lady tells her boss, making one final plea for him to not go ahead with the article.

"No, I'm giving readers what they want. Find out all you can about the crimes and talk to witnesses and victims. Put the article on my desk by closing this afternoon," Mr Oshiro says and walks off.

That evening a young man checks his watch. Two minutes to go. He is in the process of carrying groceries upstairs. After learning the time he speeds up his process.

When inside his small apartment, or shoebox as some might call this kind of residence, he quickly puts the groceries on

the kitchen bench and rushes to the radio.
He turns on the device just in time:

" . . . *more violent which is reminiscent of
thirty years ago in Northern Japan. The media
has nicknamed them the Four Little Maids.
They still seem to be very random acts, the latest
being the car yard last night. Police need your
help . . . .*"

He turns off his radio. The story is
growing more and more interesting.
Ever since the traffic light earlier that day
he can't wait to hear the news reports.
Everybody is talking excitedly about the
Four Little Maids. Everybody is wondering.
Everybody is scared.

Chapter Six

Sophie believes Kayami's husband, Shing, is a nice man. Sophie has met him on a number of occasions. Shing accompanies Rieko to her sporting events. He even cooks the nights that Kayami has work or meetings. Azuna and Fusako's husbands don't have a clue about Azuna or Fusako's movements. They are in the city all week so they are unaware of their wives weekday activities.

Kayami's husband, on the other hand, doesn't work in the city. He works from home. Shing begins to suspect something is up as Kayami arrives home from the weekly meetings a bit uptight.

Shing points out his observations.

"Your mood is changing. You come home from work late at night stressed. Not to mention you seem distant."

"I am just tired, that's all. Sorry. I'll be fine," is her planned and rehearsed response.

Shing can't ignore bruises on Kayami's arms. Nor can he ignore her growing bad temper. She is changing and he can't work out why.

Shing even hears Kayami walking around at two in the morning. Luckily for Kayami he only assumes she is getting a drink of water or going to the toilet.

Kayami talks to Miss Serizawa about her husband Wednesday night at work.

"He sees me come home late. I tell him I have been working late but I'm not sure he believes me. He read the newspaper article this afternoon about the things we have done. I think he knows I'm involved."

Miss Serizawa keeps calm and says, "He doesn't suspect a thing. Why would he think you are involved?"

As she acts nice and pleasant, reassuring Kayami, her head is filled with negative thoughts. She doesn't want this man ruining her plans. She knew this would happen eventually so now is the time to put a new plan into action.

Within a few hours Azuna and Fusako have planted a seed in Kayami's mind that Shing is cheating on Kayami with another woman. At different moments both have approached Kayami saying they have seen Shing in the company of a young lady.

Miss Serizawa is not going to put up with the fact that Kayami's husband is suspicious of something. Sooner or later he will put all the facts together and realise Kayami is out late at work the same nights that the Four Little Maids have been out committing their revenge attacks.

That night Miss Serizawa breaks into Shing and Kayami's apartment. She plants a phone number in Shing's pant pocket which will hopefully confirm the husband is cheating on Kayami and therefore he must be punished.

After work the following afternoon Sophie ducks into Miss Serizawa's office.

"See you tomorrow, Miss Serizawa."

Miss Serizawa stops opening a package of fresh seafood. This is her chance to get Sophie involved.

"Did you hear about poor Kayami?"

"Hear what?" Sophie asks.

"Oh, her husband might be seeing someone else. Isn't that horrible?" Miss Serizawa explains.

Sophie hadn't heard that before.

"Very horrible."

"He should be stopped," Miss Serizawa says.

She goes back to the box of seafood.

Sophie nods and walks out of the restaurant confused. Poor Kayami.

When Azuna's son and daughter come home late Thursday afternoon they see their mum cooking and they head upstairs to their rooms with barely a 'hello'.

They are older than Alana and Rieko. All they care about is their university homework and music. They see mum at home cooking or doing housework and assume everything is normal. They sit in their rooms studying away happily with music on.

Over at Fusako's house the story is the same with her two sons. One son only cares about fast cars. He reads car magazines or buys car parts on the Internet or draws his own car designs. He sees his mum for a short time each day and thoughts about her barely enter his head. The other son works at a bank weekdays. He wants to follow in his father's footsteps. After work, which is not far from home, he comes home to eat and sleep. They are all caught up in their own little worlds. Their interests and studies and work take over. Neither of the four would ever suspect their respective mum is a white shadowy figure at night that everyone, including themselves, is so afraid of. People are scared to go outside at night because of their mums. If the offspring ever found out the truth they would be very shocked and deny everything. They wouldn't believe the accusations.

The street lights begin to flicker on as three men meet at a park bench. They are dwarfed by the tall city buildings which surround them. The air is full of noises of commuters beginning their journeys home and this drowns out the hushed tones as the men talk of a topic of utmost importance.

"Will this stop them?" one man asks.

"Time will tell, but I'm hoping for a rift," the man in the middle says.

The third man says, "There will defiantly be a rift. At least one will surely crack. Let's just hope she will come forward and lead police to the others."

"How much do we offer them?" the first man asks.

"We don't want to offend them. The amount will have to be enough to make them want to incriminate their friends and allow for the possibility of relocating themselves and family to a safe overseas destination, if they so desire," the man in the middle says.

"Do we all agree then that the money offered will have to be ridiculous?" the third man asks.

Both of the other two nod.

"Well, what are we waiting for? I'm only here for a few more days until I set sail again so let's sort this out quickly."

The three stand and walk off in separate directions.

As the last arc of Thursday's sun dips below the horizon Mr Oshiro steps out on to his balcony. He has lived here for a few months now but he will forever love the view. Moments later the meal he has ordered from the apartment's kitchen is brought to him by a waiter.

As he eats dinner Mr Oshiro reads that afternoon's newspaper story on the Four Little Maids, which he had instructed his newest reporter to write. He is very proud of himself. And, more importantly, he was right in thinking the public would eat this story up. He had a phone call earlier from the printing department of the newspaper. They have been instructed to print fifty percent more copies to fill demand.

Mr Oshiro's body fills with endorphins from feeling so good about the article but at the same moment his throat begins to tighten. He has a drink through numbing lips. He tries to slow his breathing.

I'm just over excited, Mr Oshiro tells himself.

Seconds later he becomes dizzy, which rapidly leads to a headache.

Mr Oshiro leaves the remaining fish on the plate, goes inside and sits on his couch.

He is finding inhaling a normal breath of air to be very difficult.

Surely this panic attack will pass, I will be fine.

Minutes later he calls for an ambulance and can barely talk.

By the time apartment staff hurriedly let the ambulance officers inside Mr Oshiro's home they find him on the floor. He is alive.

"Mr Oshiro! Can you hear me?"

No response.

The ambulance officers begin to administer CPR.

"Mr Oshiro, are you with us?"

"Yes," he manages to say.

"Do you think you can stand up?"

"I will try," Mr Oshiro says.

"We will help you to the ambulance."

Mr Oshiro puts in all his effort to struggle down to the ambulance with much needed assistance. Once he is in the back of the ambulance on the way to the local hospital the officer in the back with him again performs CPR on Mr Oshiro but he soon becomes unconscious.

The doctors at the hospital perform CPR also. There is not much else that can be done.

As Mr Oshiro lays dying, struggling to get air into his lungs, he knows what has caused this. He just doesn't know *who* has caused this.

Six hours after he has eaten his dinner, Mr Oshiro is dead.

The toxicology report, which comes back within days, confirms all suspicions. Traces of tetrodotoxin were present in Mr Oshiro's system, which equates to a very horrible death.

Sophie is working at Miss Serizawa's restaurant that Friday night as usual. Her conscience is getting harder and harder to keep in a positive frame of mind. Harder and harder to keep a smile on her face. She hopes Miss Serizawa doesn't notice. She no longer likes Miss Serizawa.

Some of the topics they now talk about at the meetings at Miss Serizawa's house are frightening. Miss Serizawa may act old and sweet and innocent but Sophie can see how she has manipulated Azuna and Fusako and now Kayami into going along with her evil plans.

Revenge? Burning someone's business down to get back at the owner for bad manners is a bit too much. Now suddenly Shing is cheating on Kayami?

Sophie has met Shing. He seems like a great father and loving husband. Something is up.

Sophie is worried. She knows too much and is learning more and more about her "friend's" evil ways.

Do they want me to join them? Will I have to help burn some place down, or worse? What's in store for me? How is Miss Serizawa getting these women to do these damaging acts?

Sophie needs to come up with a way to get her and her daughter far from this place and these horrible people. In the meantime she puts up a façade and acts pleasant around them, going along with what they say so as to keep the peace.

During her shift at the restaurant she manages to avoid conversation with

Miss Serizawa. Tonight is a busy night so Sophie keeps herself occupied the whole time.

At the end of the night Sophie helps the other restaurant workers tidy the tables and chairs. Her constant thoughts are of getting away from these women. She doesn't want to be manipulated into doing something illegal.

"Goodnight, Miss Serizawa. I'm off home."

Sophie gives her and the others a little wave.

She walks to her newly acquired car and begins to drive home.

They seemed like such nice women only weeks ago. How have they become so violently minded?

As Sophie daydreams she realises a car approaching her to her left is heading straight for her car. She doesn't have time to react and swerve but does manage to brace herself. Nobody expects that a car will come out of nowhere suddenly and smash into them.

The two cars collide. Sophie is stunned. Her new car is a wreck. Before

Sophie knows what is happening two men drag her from her car. Amidst a cloud of smoke, Sophie feels something being tied around her mouth so she can't scream.

A man whispers in her ear, "Stay low."

Sophie is brought over to the car which hit hers and is placed on the back seat.

Again there is a whisper, "Lie across the seat and keep still."

The whispers are persuasive, but not in an angry way. Sophie is scared out of her wits, yet the whispering has a calming feeling present, so she obeys without much resistance. Not that she has much of a choice.

Sophie then hears talking outside the car. One voice sounds feminine, which may only be a minor detail but Sophie makes a mental note of the fact. The car doors close shortly after and they speed off.

Chapter Seven

As the car speeds along Sophie tries to listen for sounds which may help in her rescue later on, if she gets a chance to call police for help. Unfortunately, all she can make out are other cars and a distant siren for a brief moment. At one point familiar bumps on the road indicate to Sophie that they have driven over a train line, but for the most part the car speeds along without stopping once, which suggests a highway of some kind. Who knows where she is?

The car slows and Sophie guesses they have finished the journey. After a moment of feeling as if they are descending down a steep road or driveway the car finally stops.

Sophie is told to get out. She has time to see they are indoors in a car park, possibly underground, as she is rushed to an elevator door.

Before long Sophie finds herself sitting in a plain room with a desk and two vacant chairs. She assumes she is about to be questioned or interviewed. She has no idea where she is or who is about to come through the door but due to her friends involvement in some crimes lately, she concludes this will not be a friendly encounter.

She sits for what feels to her like half an hour. Sophie finds gauging time hard when just sitting in the same spot. Five minutes could have passed or fifty.

The door opens. Two men walk in.

One operates a tape player, pressing the record button, but he doesn't say a word for the entire interview.

"Hello, Sophie," the other man says.

How does he know my name? Is this a police officer?

"If I'm being charged and arrested you're meant to tell me," Sophie says.

Where has this attitude come from? But then she already knows the answer. A sudden negative attitude is likely to be caused by rising stress levels over the past few weeks. If she is arrested, who will protect her daughter from Miss Serizawa and the other evil women? She hopes the four are in neighbouring rooms along the corridor being interviewed right now too. Sophie prays they will all be arrested and locked up.

The man says, "I am a police officer. There are a few things I would like to talk to you about today, Sophie."

He shuffles a pile of paperwork.

"That's fine, but why did you have to bring me in here by crashing me off the road and forcing me into your car with a gag on?" Sophie asks.

"We don't know who is watching our movements. We don't know who is watching your movements. You were transferred to our car and brought in here so that we can talk to you without anyone out there knowing about it. A stand-in for you drove your car home and will escape via your back alleyway. Please try to understand the severity of all of this."

"Keep talking."

"You are friends with Miss Serizawa," the man begins, "and you work with Azuna, Fusako and Kayami at Miss Serizawa's restaurant. You meet with them a couple of times a week at Miss Serizawa's house."

Sophie wonders if she should be nodding in agreement.

The officer continues talking, "Miss Serizawa, Azuna, Fusako and more recently Kayami, have been involved in a number of dangerous and damaging late night activities."

He opens a folder and takes out photographs of the women.

He's been following me this whole time. I'm going to jail.

"Listen. Miss Serizawa is bad," Sophie says.

She feels now is the time to try and distance herself from the four. At this stage she is under the impression that the police department knows everything and will be arresting her shortly.

Sophie continues, "She's evil. If she learns I'm here talking to you, I and my daughter could be in serious danger."

The officer stares at Sophie.

Sophie has his attention so keeps up the performance.

"I have been trying to work out a safe method to get far away from these four women without causing conflict. You don't realise what they are capable of," Sophie says.

"We realise."

Sophie doesn't get much of a reaction from the police officer. His face has been disinterested the whole time.

"So, what happens now? Do we all go to jail?" Sophie asks.

Sophie comes across very concerned.

"You?" the officer replies. "No. You are nothing compared to Miss Serizawa. Azuna and Fusako have been joining Miss Serizawa in her transgressions for years before you and Kayami came along. Each offence has been growing more and more violent until you two have become involved. An apparent lack of activity recently means they have backed right off while you will both learn the ropes. Although there have been a few unexplained incidences lately."

"We are being trained?" Sophie asks.

She is confused.

"Oh, yes. Miss Serizawa will soon have you all doing very violent acts. From what we can tell Kayami is their current project. The way Miss Serizawa works is she will offer you something you can't refuse and by accepting her offer you are let into her little club. In return though, you must do as she says. Initiation usually involves a violent criminal act. Personally I feel you, Sophie, are a bonus. If Miss Serizawa likes you she'll make you an offer. You may become a valued member. They'll call you the Five Little Maids."

He tries to make a joke. Sophie turns pale.

"My daughter! I want to go home and make sure she is safe."

Sophie is about to stand up.

"How about we do a deal . . . ," the policeman offers in a calming voice.

"Such as . . . ?" Sophie responds in not such a calm voice.

The police officer is about to talk but he allows Sophie to go first. He can see she has an idea.

"Sort me out a replacement car to start with," she says.

"You help us catch Miss Serizawa in the act of something bad. Real bad. We'll be able to arrest her and use any evidence at the scene as a link to be able to charge her for many crimes in the past. We have never been there as she does the crime and have never found any evidence at the resulting crime scene to have a decent case against her. I'll see what I can do about a car. Now, I'll have an officer drop you home. Enter your place quietly from the alley."

"You're really serious about people watching me aren't you? I'm beginning to understand. Well you better make sure my daughter is safe," Sophie says with a firm voice.

If she is going to seriously help him Sophie wants to make sure she sets the terms.

"I will have police watch your house from now until this is over," the officer promises.

Sophie is interested, "What do I need to do?"

"How did the interview go?" the police officer's senior superintendent asks.

They are passing each other in the hallway. The police officer was hoping to avoid talking to anyone.

"She didn't say very much but she mentioned some evidence that she can remember seeing at the scene, so I'm going to check the room out now," the officer lies.

In the evidence room the officer slides a little pile of bank notes into his inner jacket pocket before leaving for the day.

Chapter Eight

"**Y**ou were hit?" Alana is astonished. "Are you alright?"

Saturday morning, after not being able to sleep, Sophie has to explain to Alana why there is a smashed up car in the driveway.

"I am fine. The crash was not too bad. The car took all of the impact," Sophie says, reassuring her daughter.

"Mum, take the day off work," Alana strongly suggests.

"Mr Nguyen will be here shortly to drop me off at a client's house."

Alana is worried, "I can't believe this. You should see a doctor."

"I'm fine Alana, please don't worry," Sophie tells her daughter.

Not long later Mr Nguyen parks out the front and, to Alana's annoyance, Sophie goes to work.

* * *

"Come in," a man calls out.

Sophie enters and shuts the door. To her surprise, and astonishment, the police officer from the interview walks in from the kitchen.

"Hello, Sophie. I need to talk to you," he says.

"Yes, and I need to talk to you," Sophie's angry attitude is back. "I need you to sort something out with my car insurance company. I'm not going to be blamed for the crash."

"I will handle the insurance claim," he says. "I need to talk with you about our interview."

"Just tell me what's going on. Who are you? I'll scream if you come near me," a worried Sophie warns.

"Don't panic. I'm Mr Quah. There are things I need to tell you that I couldn't say during the interview."

They sit opposite each other at the dining table. Sophie is reluctant at first but she should be able to trust a police officer.

"I know you're not like Miss Serizawa and the others," the police officer says. "Supposing we work together and stop Miss Serizawa, can I trust you?"

"Trust me? Can you honestly help me? Keep Miss Serizawa away from me and my daughter?"

Mr Quah notes the anxiety in her voice.

"If you help us out we might be able to," he says.

Sophie rolls her eyes, "Stick around and go along with Miss Serizawa until she does something really bad. That's the plan you mentioned in the interview. How does that help me?"

"Yes," Mr Quah says, "but there's more to the story. I couldn't say very much yesterday. I have not told anybody this. Years ago I was living in Shanghai. I had a motorbike accident. After hospital I started having acupuncture, with an old lady, to help relieve the pain of traction. One time I was lying on the bed with the needles in my back and neck and the old lady began talking. She grew up on the mountain slopes which are now all houses. Life was very different back then.

As a child she heard a myth about a young lady that lived on one of those mountains years earlier. This young lady would go down the mountain every so often and seek out a bad man from the city and kill him. The acupuncturist's tale was very strange. After the needles were pulled out of my neck and back I felt as though my visions were perhaps a dream so I didn't ask her to elaborate. Not long later I moved to Japan and forgot all about her. I trained to be a police officer and have been ever since."

Sophie has been listening the whole time and fails to know how the information concerns her.

"Where does Miss Serizawa come into this story?" Sophie asks. "And how do I fit in?"

"Eight years ago," Mr Quah starts another story, "I helped a detective for a few months when I was starting out as an officer. I came across a file on unsolved murders. I read one that sounded similar to the story the old acupuncturist had told me about. I've been secretly researching the murders ever since. I cut short my holiday so I can spend more time trying to piece together the similarities and solve this. Luckily my superintendent thinks that I have taken my annual leave and he is allowing me to come in and work on some other cases."

"I'm lost. What happens now?"

Sophie can't understand where she and Miss Serizawa are involved.

Mr Quah goes into another room and comes back with an old file.

As he returns to the dining table he says, "This might help to explain what's going on."

He hands Sophie a black and white sketch. The paper is creased and scratched but Sophie can see the sketching is of a woman.

"Yes," Sophie says, "this is Miss Serizawa. Well the image looks like her, maybe twenty years ago or more."

"Roughly a hundred and eighty years ago," Mr Quah says.

Sophie focuses her eyes on the sketch again.

"So this person is Miss Serizawa's grandmother?" Sophie asks.

"This came with a police file from Singapore written in 1826. Before the 1890s photographs would fade so people would quickly trace the image before it disappeared. The Singapore police were watching this woman for some time until she vanished," Mr Quah explains.

"What happened to her?" Sophie asks.

"I guess she moved and changed names," he says.

Mr Quah hands Sophie another small piece of paper that is in a plastic sleeve.

On the old paper is a nearly faded drawing.

Mr Quah explains, "This was apparently drawn in Venice in the 1500's from a soldier's description. As you can see the drawing shows a woman dressed in traditional oriental clothes. On the back of the paper is written the name 'Zhu-Ku'. I haven't been able to find out much about her except that a past relative of the same name may have killed an emperor in China many years earlier, but disappeared before being caught."

"The lady resembles Miss Serizawa a little bit, if I squint," Sophie laughs and hands back the drawing. "This is all very silly. What's the point of this?"

"The drawing of the lady in 1500's Venice was among the 1826 Singapore police reports. I reckon they were on to something. I think they had some evidence or a lead that the women were related. And both very dangerous. They were being pursued for some reason of other. I assume the police gave up after their suspect vanished."

"You have no doubt Miss Serizawa is the descendent. She is the great granddaughter of this Zhu-Ku?" Sophie asks.

"I believe she is," Mr Quah replies. "You may have heard about some trouble in northern Japan three decades ago. The police there had a tough time trying to catch a group of people terrorising citizens. Innocent people died but there were never any convictions. When I started investigating this eight years ago I went on a holiday to northern Japan to research events. I read as many files as I could get my hands on. Nothing jumped out at me. Over the past few months little crimes have started up here. Everyone at the police station is so sure with themselves that teenagers are causing this trouble and that the violence and damage will stop soon but I have been walking the streets at night trying to spot anything remotely similar to what happened in the North. I have seen a woman on a few occasions but lost her again. Then weeks later I saw more women. Again they disappear before I get close. After weeks of stalking these women, who are lurking in the shadows at night, I feel I can say I know who they are and I have a feeling they are preparing themselves for major assaults."

Mr Quah wonders if he should be telling Sophie all of this but there has to be trust between them.

"What do we do now?" Sophie says, trying to remain calm.

"What happens now," Mr Quah answers, "is that we need to find a way to stop Miss Serizawa for good. The plan I've told my supervisor is basic. I want to go further than merely arresting Miss Serizawa for some little crime. I am definitely not letting her get away like the police did to Miss Serizawa's relatives in the past, if they are related."

Sophie agrees, "I don't think we should let her get away lightly. But stopping her by normal methods does not really seem to be a possibility."

Mr Quah nods, "To be honest I've been thinking the same thing. Being violent while seeking revenge is in her blood. She's smart too, never been caught before. The authorities will find stopping her hard. Hard to make her want to be a good citizen, even after rehabilitation."

"Well I suggest the first thing we do is find out more about Miss Serizawa's relatives. Like Zhu-Ku. What happened to her? How did she commit crimes? How did she manage to evade police?"

Mr Quah agrees, "If we find out about Miss Serizawa's past relatives and get any clue as to how police stopped them or whether they ever became part of normal society, this might give us a way to stop Miss Serizawa for good."

Mr Quah is excited. Finally he has someone to talk to about this who will try and help him stop Miss Serizawa after all this time.

"I went to a bookstore not long ago," Sophie recalls. "If I can find the correct laneway again the shop would be a good place to start looking for information. The place was full of interesting old books from what I saw. I picked one up and read a passage mentioning evil genes. I think that's what the words were saying. I still can't read Japanese very well. I know nothing about genetics but from my understanding of the paragraph there can exist these violent genes that come down the line, generation to generation, much stronger than any normal hereditary gene."

Mr Quah has been listening very closely.

"We'll try and find a directory of some kind. A listing of old families. We could also try to find other books mentioning evil genes which are passed from generation to generation and see if there is any truth behind it."

Sophie writes down where the shopping district is located. They both agree to meet outside the tram station with the fountain in the morning.

"See you tomorrow," Sophie says to Mr Quah.

As Sophie leaves Mr Quah hands her a pile of money.

He mutters to himself, "I came across this the other day."

Sophie stares at the money in her hand.

"What do I do with this?" Sophie asks suspiciously.

"The police crashed your car so the police will help you to buy a new one," he says, smiling to himself.

That night Sophie cooks dinner and talks to her daughter.

"Has anybody been following you at all?" Sophie asks.

She is still shaken up by recent events.

Alana is a little bit scared by the question.

"No, why? What's happened?" she asks.

Sophie replies, "My new friends might not be as normal, nor as nice, as we thought. I'm just worried."

She stops cooking and turns to her daughter. Alana notices her troubled expression.

"Mum," Alana says, rolling her eyes, "what now? Why worry? I thought everything was great."

Sophie stops frowning.

"Everything is great. Just be careful. Don't talk to anyone," she says.

Alana rolls her eyes again.

"Promise me you'll be careful, Alana."

Sophie speaks firmly which scares her daughter.

"I promise, Mum."

"You left her there like a wounded animal."

A woman stands over a cowering man.

"Please don't hurt me," he begs.

"How would you like to feel what she felt? All alone, knowing the end was coming," she doesn't hear his whimpers.

"Please!" He looks to the two women standing close behind their leader. "I don't want to feel what she felt. I . . . ."

"Do you realize the pain she would have been in? You should have an idea of what she went through," the leader tells the frightened man.

"No! Please, you can't run a car over me. That is horrible!"

"Yes, that would be very horrible. But you have misunderstood me, Mr Masatoshi."

The two women step forward and pick the man up like he is filled with stuffing. They throw him out of the fourth floor window. He lands on a car parked down below. The woman in charge bursts out laughing and leaves the room wiping the tears from her eyes. Her friends scurry along after her.

Chapter Nine

Early the next morning, after acting happy during Tai Chi, Sophie catches the tram to meet Mr Quah. As she hops off the tram Sophie sees him waiting by the fountain eating something. To Sophie he is mysterious. He never seems to draw attention to himself. Sophie doubts he cares what people think about him.

"Good morning," Mr Quah says when he sees Sophie approach.

He closes a plastic container that only minutes ago held half a dozen rambutans.

Sophie can't help but notice Mr Quah always dresses well. She has noticed his designer jacket. He has neat hair and nice pants every time she sees him but he's so down to earth. He is fairly tall and seems quite athletic.

Sophie puts her mind back on track.

"I think we go down that way," she says.

Sophie points towards a busy and narrow street in the distance. They begin walking. Sophie can't tell how old Mr Quah is. She guesses he is in his mid-thirties but he could be ten years younger or even near to fifty. Sophie stops walking. She thought the bookstore was down this narrow alley but she is wrong. They make a left turn and Sophie feels as if she has walked in a circle. All the little streets look identical. All the little shops look identical. Luckily Sophie spots the furniture shop.

"The bookstore is this way," she says.

Her spirits quickly pick up.

They turn right. Finally they find the correct street. This time Sophie takes notice of the lane's sign which translates to Origin Alley. As they walk further along they spot the bookstore.

"We're too early," Mr Quah says as Sophie sits down to wait.

"The place will open in ten minutes," Sophie says, checking her watch.

Sophie and Mr Quah talk about their plan.

"As far as Miss Serizawa is concerned," Mr Quah explains to Sophie, "nothing is different. Do as you normally do. We'll try to meet up once a day. I'll rent a different apartment each time we are to meet. I'll call your boss with a new name and request you to clean the house. That way we can keep in touch without anyone knowing. As soon as you hear that Miss Serizawa is planning one of her big revenge attacks tell me right away."

"I will," she says.

Sophie is not one hundred percent keen on the idea.

Not long later the bookstore opens and they walk inside.

Sophie shows Mr Quah where the books were that had caught her eye.

"They were really detailed. Scary sketches and amazing calligraphy all over the pages. I didn't have the time to read them properly though."

Mr Quah grins, "We'll find them."

He sets off to investigate.

They search through shelves and piles of old books. Sophie can't find the one she saw last time she was in the shop. They find old textbooks, books about herbs used for medicines, old encyclopaedias, cookbooks and children's stories from long ago.

"We need older books. These are one hundred years old at the most," Mr Quah says.

He goes and finds the shopkeeper.

"We are searching for an older book," Mr Quah tells the man standing behind the front counter.

The shopkeeper points them to a small room.

"Older and rare books kept in there, behind glass," he says.

As Sophie and Mr Quah walk to a rear room Sophie says, "I didn't go in here last time. The book is long gone, but we'll have a look."

The glass cabinet does contain very old books. Mr Quah guesses some may even be over 300 or 400 years old. "They will crumble into dust if dropped," Mr Quah says.

"The book I saw last time is not here," Sophie feels beaten.

They have no plan B.

Mr Quah sees Sophie's sadness growing. She is normally very positive.

Mr Quah approaches the shopkeeper again.

"You were selling an old book here not long ago," Mr Quah explains to the man. "My friend liked what she saw and tried reading a bit. We are after any similar books perhaps mentioning myths about evil genes being passed on to the next generation. Do you know any information about that book, or have any item similar?"

To the relief of Mr Quah and Sophie the shopkeeper pauses and searches his brain for a response that may help.

He finally says, "Any book mentioning evil genes is highly sought after. There are a few collectors. I've heard one or two actually burn them. They don't want that sort of information in the hands of the public as that type of subject matter is against their religion. I do know of a temple in northern China that has a collection. They might be the best place to try. The others are all private collections as far as I know."

He writes down the name of the Chinese temple.

"Thank you very much," Sophie says.

She is about to walk out but quickly asks, "If you remember the book I saw, do you remember who came in and bought it?"

"I don't know the person. I have seen them once before. They bought another book like you described. Something about them was odd. They did not seem excited. I think buying the book made them mad. Normally a collector, or even an ordinary customer, is happy to purchase a book and are looking forward to reading it so if there is no emotion I find that strange."

Sophie wonders to herself, 'The person probably burnt the books. Like the man said—against their religion.'

Mr Quah and Sophie walk together to the tram stop.

"I suppose I have to travel to China," Mr Quah tells Sophie.

"Really?" Sophie asks.

Mr Quah nods, "You heard the shopkeeper. Any book mentioning evil genes goes straight to private collections. We don't even know who the people are. We would have to find that out somehow. My best bet is the Temple in China."

"Our best bet. I'm coming with you. Hopefully they can help us."

Mr Quah doesn't know what to say. He knows Sophie is strong willed and wants her daughter to be safe. He wasn't expecting Sophie to want to travel with him.

As Mr Quah and Sophie continue walking down the narrow old shopping lanes, they agree to meet the next day and talk the details over.

Chapter Ten

"China," Sophie says.

"Why?" Alana asks.

Sophie and Alana are sitting at the kitchen table eating dinner. Sophie has told Alana everything.

"They might have information that will stop Miss Serizawa, and the others, from being so evil," Sophie explains.

Alana says, "Can't you just let the police deal with this?"

Sophie can see her daughter is scared. Alana doesn't want her mum being mixed up in all this.

"The police don't know the extent of the situation," Sophie tells Alana. "All they want to do is arrest Miss Serizawa. That is only if she ever does something bad enough, not to mention she has to leave evidence or get caught in the act. She's very smart."

"I hope you're smarter," Alana says under her breath.

* * *

Early in the morning Sophie knocks at an apartment door. She is dressed as a cleaner so if anyone is following her nothing unusual is happening to arouse suspicion. As planned, Mr Quah opens the door to greet her.

Mr Quah is paying Sophie's boss, Mr Nguyen, as a client, so to Mr Nguyen, and more importantly to Miss Serizawa, Sophie appears to still be working as normal.

Inside Mr Quah and Sophie sit down to work out what the next step is.

"How can I go to China? Miss Serizawa will know. She will be on to me," Sophie says, knowing that trying to fool Miss Serizawa will be risky.

She really wants to go and help Mr Quah but now has doubts.

Mr Quah replies, "I've been thinking. Fake an illness. Or accident. Take some time off work. I know a doctor who could write a note for you. I'll have police watch your home too, like we talked about, to make sure your daughter is safe."

"I'm not sure that Miss Serizawa will believe I'm sick," Sophie says, "but there are probably not many other options."

Mr Quah takes this as her agreement to come to China and hands Sophie a passport.

She opens the passport and sees her picture inside.

"What's this?" she asks.

"I used the picture the station took when you were brought in for questioning."

Sophie sees that her name has been changed.

"False passport?" Sophie questions Mr Quah.

He says quietly, "A friend owed me a favour. Nobody will be able to tell."

Sophie is unsure of that but puts the passport into her handbag.

"When shall we go? Do you have any plans over the next week?" Mr Quah asks.

Mr Quah really wants to hurry things along.

"Work and work. I'll go to work tonight at the restaurant and act as if I am coming down with an illness. Plant the seed. See how Miss Serizawa reacts."

"Excellent," Mr Quah says. "I will make the travel bookings this afternoon. We will fly to China early one morning, visit the temple and fly back that night. Now, we can't sit together or even look at each other. We don't want anyone tailing us to know we're together."

Sophie nods and says, "Let's keep our fingers crossed that we find some book with any information about evil genes."

Sophie doesn't want this to be a waste of time.

"What do you imagine Miss Serizawa is exactly?" Mr Quah asks Sophie.

Sophie really isn't sure what to think.

She says, "Umm, well I guess the evil has been passed on somehow from the great great great grandmother in the 1500's to the great grandmother in 1826 and now the gene is in Miss Serizawa. Whether we can extract that evil from Miss Serizawa and make her normal we'll have to wait and see."

Mr Quah adds, "I know this is a very strange state of affairs. I stop every now and then and can't believe this situation."

Sophie stands and Mr Quah walks her out.

"It'll be over soon," she says.

* * *

"What shall I write for you?"

Sophie is in the doctor's office that afternoon getting a note for absence. She is the only patient and all the other employees have left long ago.

"Write I have something contagious," she tells the doctor. "I don't want any visitors."

She wants at least two days off work. The doctor pauses for a moment and then starts writing.

"You have a new strain of flu," he explains. "The bacteria have just struck our country weeks ago so the virus hasn't spread very much yet. I will write out a fake form for you to take to the pharmacist so you can show anyone tailing you that you are picking up medication. I have written an absence form for your employer covering you for three days. If you need more time come back and see me."

Sophie thanks the nice doctor for his help.

"Tell Mr Quah I say hello," he says as he shows Sophie out.

* * *

During her shift at Miss Serizawa's restaurant Sophie tries to come across as though she is ill. She is careful not to overdo the act. Halfway through her shift she sneaks into the kitchen supply room and sniffs chilli powder. Minutes later Miss Serizawa sees Sophie sneezing multiple times. Sophie acts as if everything is fine and keeps working. Azuna approaches Sophie.

Azuna says, "If you are feeling ill you can go home."

Sophie sniffles.

"Are you sure?" Sophie asks. "I don't want Miss Serizawa to be annoyed with me leaving and her being one staff down."

"For hygiene reasons you can't be sick around food," Azuna explains.

Sophie already knows this. She almost smiles as her eyes fill with water, reacting to the chilli powder.

"Sorry. I'll go home. Tell Miss Serizawa I'm very sorry. I must have an allergy or something like that."

Sophie leaves for home. She looks a mess. The plan is in action.

* * *

That night Sophie rings Miss Serizawa and also calls Mr Nguyen at the cleaning company and informs them both of her illness.

"Yes, the virus is highly contagious unfortunately," she tells Miss Serizawa with a sniffle.

Mr Nguyen is fine with her taking time off.

His encouraging, but loud, words to her are, "You no worry."

Both wish her well.

All Sophie can do now is wait for Mr Quah to somehow get in touch with her to let her know about the China adventure.

Sophie sits quietly flicking through her evening newspaper. A brochure falls on the floor. Sophie picks up the loose piece of paper, thinking nothing of it, but realises something is tucked away in the brochure. Mr Quah has put the plane tickets to and from China in Sophie's morning paper. The plane departs early the next morning.

She goes and talks to Alana.

"Go to school and come home later as if nothing is up. No one can know I'm going away for the day. You will have undercover police keeping an eye on you so don't worry."

"I'm more worried about you."

Sophie wishes her daughter a goodnight and then goes and packs a small bag.

Chapter Eleven

Before sunrise the next morning Sophie sneaks out of her house and catches a bus to the airport. Sophie doesn't have any luggage to check in at the departure counters so she walks straight to the gate and soon after boards her flight to Beijing.

Sophie is nervous. She waits in her seat on the place without seeing Mr Quah. Has he made it to the plane?

She tried looking for Mr Quah at the airport but didn't see him there either.

As the plane shoots up into the sky Sophie sits back in her seat and attempts to read a magazine. This proves pointless. Throughout the flight her only thoughts are all related to Miss Serizawa, the temple and the safety of Alana.

Hours later Sophie's plane lands at Beijing Airport. She follows the other passengers until she sees an exit.

Still no sign of Mr Quah as she finds the tourist bus that goes up to the temple. Reluctantly she climbs aboard.

Miss Serizawa, Azuna, Fusako and Kayami would be finishing their Tai Chi right now, she imagines as she sets her watch back an hour.

Sophie daydreams as she sits on a small tourist bus in China heading for the mountains where an old temple will hopefully have ancient books with pages containing information that will stop an evil gene that is in Miss Serizawa.

How did I end up here? She wonders if she has lost her mind. And where is Mr Quah?

She remembers their conversation and one of his promises, "In Beijing catch a bus with other tourists to the temple. I will be with you all the way."

During the two-hour bumpy journey Sophie observes the other passengers on the small bus. She counts at least fifteen people. Mostly older adults. One elderly couple has two young children. Sophie suspects the couple has persuaded their grandchildren to come along on this journey.

As the small tourist bus rounds a cliff Sophie sees the temple in the distance. The view is amazing. She wishes she had packed a camera. Out of the window Sophie can see a cliff to the left and on the right the dirt road clutches the mountain which reaches up to the clouds. The old temple nestles in the middle of this tranquil scene.

Within minutes the bus slows outside the temple. Sophie's heart begins to race. Everyone becomes excited as they exit the bus but Sophie's excitement is for a different reason. She isn't here as a tourist.

Sophie feels lonely as she watches the empty bus drive back down the mountain. She turns to walk as an old man from the bus approaches her.

"Sophie," he whispers.

"Yes?"

Sophie wonders how he knew her name, and then realises.

"Don't say anything," Mr Quah says, pretending to dig around in his backpack for something.

Sophie finds his disguise amusing but restrains herself from letting her hysteria show.

They walk inside as she remembers that this 'old man' had been with her the entire journey. She saw an old man at the airport in Japan. An old man was sitting four seats in front of her on the plane.

"Act like we're talking about the temple and becoming touristy pals," he whispers again.

"Yes, I like the eaves too," Sophie says. "The detail on the carvings is amazing."

A tour guide comes over to their group.

"Welcome everybody."

Everybody says hello. One or two take photos of the tour guide for their relatives and friends to view when they return from their holidays.

The tour guide says, "This temple was constructed and built back during . . . ."

Sophie stops listening. She wants to get to the library.

Two drawn-out hours later the tour ends. No sign of the old library although a light lunch was provided which was nice.

Sophie has been acting interested. There are lots of facts and scenery to be interested about. But deep down all she wants to do is read. They are wasting time. Being so close to some possible answers is frustrating her.

Mr Quah, in his disguise, has been walking with her for most of the tour. He talks to a few of the other tourists so onlookers will believe that he is just a friendly old man and him talking to Sophie is quite innocent. An old man on a tour talking to a lady who has similar interests in an ancient temple as he does.

After the tour Sophie finds herself sitting outside the temple alone watching the bus slowly drive up the mountain towards her. This will drop off a fresh, new load of excited tourists for the evening tour while taking Sophie's tired group back down to the city.

Mr Quah comes and sits with her.

"I've organized for you and me to take the later bus back down the mountain so we have a bit of time to search the library."

"Are they letting us read the books?" Sophie asks.

"Yes, I told the temple staff you are my niece and that an old relative of ours from hundreds of years ago is mentioned in an ancient book that lives here," Mr Quah is very pleased with himself.

"Excellent. I've been dying to get to the library," Sophie says, jumping up.

The library is located on the opposite side of the temple grounds. As she walks Sophie takes in her peaceful surroundings. She does like the pagodas and walled gardens.

"Such a shame that we are here on business and not able to enjoy the place," she tells Mr Quah.

Sophie and Mr Quah arrive at a courtyard. To their left is a prayer room. To their right is the living area for visiting monks. Straight ahead is the old library which is usually only reserved for monks to learn from the ancient text.

Sophie and Mr Quah enter the library and an old monk greets them.

"I didn't expect the place to be so big. There must be millions of books here," Sophie says.

"Can you please show us to old books from Japan," Mr Quah asks the monk.

He walks Sophie and Mr Quah through the library and shows them where to begin looking.

"Please be careful with the pages," he adds and walks away.

Sophie and Mr Quah make their way to the shelves.

"We should probably have cotton gloves," Mr Quah says.

"I would hate to drop a book. We have a limited amount of time here so let's split up," Sophie whispers.

Mr Quah agrees and Sophie walks around the corner.

Where do I start?

After inspecting the shelves very closely for ten minutes she realises there is no specific order. Everything appears to be mixed up. Perhaps a regular visitor will learn where certain books are kept but she is lost.

She picks up another book and scans the pages. Nothing jumps out at her. Next book. Nothing.

Shelves later and still nothing. She hasn't heard a word from Mr Quah so Sophie guesses he's having as much fun as her.

At one stage Sophie's eyes spot the name Zhu-Ku but she loses her place on the page. All the scanning of the pages has made her eyes go blurry.

"Mr Quah," she calls out.

He comes around the corner seconds later carrying a book.

"I've found the name 'Zhu-Ku' in a book but lost my spot on the page," she tells him. "Wait, here it is. Lan Zhu-Ku was betrayed by the emperor. She disappeared and no one heard from her again. The townspeople believe she was ashamed that her husband committed adultery. The emperor died months later, murdered. The assassin was never found."

Sophie stops reading.

"Lan Zhu-Ku," Mr Quah says to himself.

Finally after all this time he knows her name.

"The article doesn't mention a child," Sophie says.

Mr Quah points to the book in his hands.

"That's similar to something I found in this book," Mr Quah says, "which lists mothers who have given birth out of wedlock, most of whom ran away from town. Here is a paragraph saying about a woman who ran away from her husband and secretly gave birth to her daughter in the mountains. The female baby is raised by the mother with the view of hating all men. The mother's first lesson to the child is to bring her along to watch while the mother gets revenge on her next male victim. I don't really want to know what the revenge involves."

Mr Quah looks at Sophie and then keeps reading, "Every generation is the same. The first female baby is raised with the same hatred to males."

"How do we know these stories are fact and not fiction?" Sophie says.

Mr Quah shudders at the thought of the revenge attack.

"I don't know," he says, "but if they are real where is the justification? Are these stories even connected?"

"What if you have been right all along? Miss Serizawa is the descendant of these women. She will have to get pregnant soon and have a daughter to raise as her own if she wants to continue the tradition. Considering Miss Serizawa's age I can't see how that is likely."

Mr Quah says, "To me it seems as if the hatred towards men is, over the generations, ever increasing. The feelings of revenge might not need to be planted into the child now. They might just be there in the brain. The thoughts, feelings and actions of the daughters may have become instinct."

Sophie reads the last line on the page that Mr Quah is still holding open.

"The father," she says, "is unaware of the bond between mother and daughter and goes about his life believing he is part of a normal everyday household."

"Scary," Mr Quah says. "These women seek revenge for something that was done a thousand years ago, or more, and take their anger out on innocent males. Why did I ever stick my nose into this case?"

Mr Quah and Sophie walk around the library until they find a monk to talk to.

Mr Quah asks, "Do you know anything about this myth?"

The monk reads the passage and says, "I have heard this before. As boy I was told this. Part of bedtime story. Be nice to your sister or evil woman come at night and get you. Parents named them 'Night Shade' family."

"Like the poisonous plants?" Sophie laughs.

The monk has a worried expression on his face while he says, "Don't laugh. This not funny story. Every boy that hears story very scared. Gave me nightmare."

He walks off.

"I think I offended him," Sophie says.

"This is all very strange," Mr Quah says as he shuts the book.

They put the books back on the shelves and walk away from the library.

Sophie and Mr Quah hardly say a word as they sit and wait for the bus ride back into the town. They have given up. Even though the bus to town won't be there to pick the tourist group up for an hour Sophie and Mr Quah are more confused than when they arrived at the temple so they sit and wait quietly. Both feel somewhat defeated.

Alana sits in the lounge room with the radio on. She gave up on television hours ago. There isn't much else she can do. She can't go out anywhere.

Alana wonders how obvious the police out the front look. She feels like she is under house arrest.

The only good thing to come out of this is a few days off school.

At that moment a news story catches Alana's ears:

"*. . . the payment offered has been increased by the government and we again must stress that any information at all given by the public regarding these four little maids will be much appreciated by the authorities. Reward will be paid if an arrest arises from your call . . . .*"

This is news to Alana.

A tiny part of Alana almost believes that the police may close in on these women with attempts, like the reward, to get the public involved. But the rest of Alana knows stopping the women will not be that easy. She doesn't get her hopes up.

Chapter Twelve

"**E**xcuse me."

Mr Quah and Sophie jump slightly and turn around.

A monk is standing over them.

"I'm sorry for disturbing your meditation," the monk says.

"Oh, we're just waiting for the bus," Sophie replies.

"I saw you talking and asking questions," the monk says. "You seek information. You won't be able to find the information here."

"Can you help us?" Mr Quah doesn't have a clue as to what this monk is on about but wants to get any help he can.

"I cannot," the monk says, shaking his head from side to side, "and no book will have the answers you need."

Sophie grows restless but remains calm.

"Who can help us?" she asks the monk.

"Your problem is over two thousand years old," the monk explains. "The oldest books in the world are not going to be of use. Stories and myths cannot help you. Find someone who was there."

'Great, now we have to time travel,' Sophie says quietly to herself.

Mr Quah keeps the monk talking by asking, "Who was there?"

"The only help I can offer is telling you a mountain name," the monk says. "If you can find the mountain this will be your pathway to understanding."

"What is the mountain's name?" Mr Quah asks.

"Yue Shan," the old monk says and walks off.

Now they have to find the mountain.

Sophie and Mr Quah walk to the small entry booth and ask a temple guide for a street directory.

Sophie flicks through the index.

"Nothing comes up as Yue Shan," she says to Mr Quah.

Mr Quah searches the pages of mountainous countryside. He can't find the name either.

"A mountain from two thousand years ago or more might not be there now. We need really old maps."

Sophie and Mr Quah rush back to the library. They only have half an hour to find the location of Yue Shan.

Mr Quah goes straight to the monk from earlier, who is busy reading.

"Sorry to bother you again, but can you point me in the direction of Chinese maps, geography?" Mr Quah asks.

The monk is happy to help and shows Sophie and Mr Quah exactly where old maps can be found.

"Thank you very much," both say to the monk.

Before long they come across an old map that shows farmland and rivers in the north of the country.

"There!" Mr Quah spots the name Yue Shan.

Sophie studies the map, "So the mountain is west of the city, a few hours drive."

"We'll get up early and be there by breakfast tomorrow."

"I feel bad for being apart from Alana," Sophie says.

"Give her a phone call while I try and change our plane tickets at the airport," Mr Quah says.

Mr Quah and Sophie are happy with the new information they have found in the library. They catch their tour bus back into town while the sun sets in the distance, bringing another day to an end.

At the Beijing Airport that night after a quick take-away meal Sophie calls her daughter while Mr Quah goes and gets the plane tickets altered.

"Alana," Sophie says when her daughter answers the phone. "How is everything?"

There is panic in Sophie's voice.

Alana reassures her mum by saying, "Everything is fine. Nobody has come looking for you. Are you about to fly home?"

"We have to go to a mountain tomorrow," Sophie explains. "Someone there can help us. I hope. We will fly home tomorrow night."

Sophie hates being away from her daughter but remains strong.

Alana asks, "Why are you staying there longer? I'm scared to be here alone."

The China visit was supposed to be a quick trip. Alana only acted brave because she thought her mum was about to fly home.

"We will only be in the province for a few hours. They might know how to stop Miss Serizawa. Sorry I can't come home now."

Sophie puts another coin in the pay phone.

"I really hope I don't get any visitors," Alana says as she scans all the dark shadows in the room.

Sophie hopes Alana doesn't get any visitors too.

"I doubt that," Sophie says. "They all believe I'm sick in bed. They don't want to catch my contagious germs."

Alana laughs.

"They might think I have caught the virus off you and stay away for that reason too," Alana says.

Sophie adds, "Remember, there is a police officer out the front so please don't worry."

"I know. Oh, and I heard the authorities have offered money to pay the public for any information leading to an arrest," Alana informs her mum.

"Really? I don't think that will help. The four little maids travel around like ghosts. That is how they have managed to escape the law for so long. Of course the police and the government need to act like they are doing all they can, and good luck to them. I will call you tomorrow Alana, just before our flight departs from here. Take care, Alana. See you soon," Sophie tells her daughter.

"Goodbye, Mum. Good luck," Alana quickly adds.

Sophie hangs up and turns to go looking for Mr Quah.

"I've hired a car for tomorrow. I have also given a hotel down the road a call and booked us rooms each for the night. And here is your new plane ticket for tomorrow night," Mr Quah says when he finds Sophie.

Sophie follows Mr Quah as he walks outside to find a taxi, each deep in thought.

Mr Quah has been keeping an eye out for anyone tailing them but he hasn't noticed anything unusual. He doesn't worry about wearing his disguise and the freedom of being able to walk around together allows Sophie and him to concentrate on more pressing matters. Neither knows exactly what to expect tomorrow.

Who are we meeting with? How can this person stop Miss Serizawa?

The taxi ride to the hotel lasts ten minutes. Both remain quiet the whole time. Sophie watches the scenery go past, barely blinking, until the taxi slows down outside a very tall glass skyscraper.

Sophie and Mr Quah check into their hotel rooms. Sophie can't help but notice the mood in the air. The feeling of failure has gone but there is still an almost negative air hovering over them. Fear of the unknown, she assumes.

Tomorrow morning they will make an early start to the mountain, so Sophie gets ready for bed and is asleep within minutes. Next door, Mr Quah lays awake wondering a million things. He has been interested in this myth for many years and wonders if he will soon have enough answers to be able to put all the pieces of this puzzle together. If the stories and myths are true, as the monk believes them to be, this may be a two thousand year old mystery.

Mr Quah can't believe it. He knows the Chinese police in 1826 must have been close. They had a partial name and a drawing from the authorities of the 1500s of a possible female suspect. Something stopped them. Whether they had all the pieces, Mr Quah will never know. If only they knew what was happening now. Mr Quah hopes he can solve this thing and give all involved, from the past and present, much needed peace.

Chapter Thirteen

Sophie and Mr Quah stand at the edge of a massive foggy lake.

The sun has only just risen and all they can see in front of them is low-lying cloud.

The two are wearing jackets to keep the damp and icy morning air at bay.

"Where's the mountain?" Sophie asks.

Mr Quah recalls what he saw at the library, "The map said Yue Shan should be right in front of us. I'll go to that little old farm house there and ask them."

Mr Quah hurries off to a house which is further along the lake.

Sophie sits down to wait for him, hugging herself for warmth. She feels like they are on a wild goose-chase. The temple seems to have been a waste of time because now she waits by a lake where a mountain should be.

Meanwhile her daughter is in danger.

Why didn't I bring Alana with me?

She can't wait to be home.

Mr Quah runs back to Sophie.

"This was all fertile farmland apparently," Mr Quah explains. "Long ago there used to be towns here but they built a dam wall further down-stream and this region has been flooded ever since. Thousands of villagers had to relocate."

"So much for finding someone here to help us," Sophie says.

They turn and walk back to their hire car.

Sophie climbs in. Just as Mr Quah climbs in next to her Sophie sees something.

"Look there," Sophie says, pointing at the lake.

Mr Quah stares out at the foggy water.

"Where am I looking?" he asks.

Mr Quah squints, bobbing his head up and down, as he gazes out into the bright white cloud.

Sophie points excitedly.

"Just there! The clouds resemble a mountain. That's a bit odd."

"Only a coincidence," Mr Quah says as he turns the car ignition on.

"I want to check. Come on," Sophie says.

She climbs back out of the car. With little choice, Mr Quah turns off the car ignition and follows.

Sophie calls out, "We have come this far!"

Two hundred metres along the lakes edge is a small boat tied up to an old wood jetty. Mr Quah notes the rotting beams and steps lightly.

"Let's borrow this and have a closer inspection of the middle of the lake," Sophie suggests. "Who knows what's out there."

Mr Quah isn't very positive about this idea. Reluctantly he follows Sophie into the boat as it sways to and fro.

He takes the oars and starts to row. Minutes later he has had enough. An hour later his arm muscles are burning. He doesn't talk the whole time. He is too busy battling with his brain which wanted to give up long ago. When he lifts his head up, slowly because of the jarring stiffness in his neck, he sees his reward. A massive mountain rises out from the lake.

"Here we are then," he says happily, as if nothing is out of the ordinary.

Sophie jumps out of the boat and on to the rocky mountain base.

Mr Quah stumbles out of the boat, one foot slips into the water, and he ties the boat rope to a nearby tree.

Mr Quah can't help but notice that his luck is fading while Sophie is leading the way full steam ahead. She is on a roll. She knows in her heart something good will happen very soon.

On a city train packed with commuters heading to work a man stands equidistant from either end of the carriage. He hates being stuck in the middle of the carriage like this. He doesn't like to admit to himself that he is claustrophobic but this tests him.

The price to pay for wanting to mix with society, he says to himself.

Work would easily organise a driver to pick him up every morning from his home in a heartbeat but he chooses to spend time with common man.

As the man walks from the train out on to the street he checks his watch. Now four minutes behind schedule. He picks up his pace to make the green light at the pedestrian crossing but the light goes red before he can get to cross.

All he can do is watch the traffic stream past.

When the lights go green for the pedestrians to cross he checks his watch as he walks. He can see his building. One more pedestrian crossing and he will be at the entrance to his workplace. The light is red for him but after a quick check for cars he decides to take the risk and walk. Not a good example for the Chief of the Metropolitan Police Department to be setting.

At that moment there is a loud noise and the man watches his office windows blow out and fall more than twenty floors to the pavement below. Nothing prepares a person for this. The helpless onlookers, including himself, take a moment to react as processing what has just happened right before their eyes is not easy.

The Chief of the Metropolitan Police Department rushes to help the injured, hoping a witness is on the phone to the emergency services. Luckily most pedestrians had time to run out of the way. Only after tending to the worst of the injured does he realise he hasn't even thought about the well being of his co-workers up in his office.

From what Sophie and Mr Quah can see there is no sign of human life on the island. No sign of bird life nor animal either. The only life is the trees. Further up the slope the fog may thin out to reveal more hospitable terrain.

Sophie begins to follow a path that seems to be going in an upward direction.

"I think that path is from rainfalls," Mr Quah says, but she's already walking.

He trails after Sophie since there are no other paths to follow.

"I guess we see where it goes," Mr Quah mutters.

They keep a steady pace as they ascend the mountain. The fog becomes thinner so now they can see for fifty metres in front of them rather than twenty. The rocky path winds up further and further into the sky. Mr Quah has no doubt they are walking up a water way caused by rain rushing down the slope but he doesn't complain out loud.

He wonders if anyone else is on this island. Maybe nobody ever comes here.

After nearly two hours of walking up the mountainside, Sophie spots what looks like a hut that has become visible in the distance.

She says, "I wonder if anyone's home today."

Sophie increases her pace.

Mr Quah smiles and says, "Who delivers their mail?"

He is trying to keep himself entertained but hurries along.

As Sophie gets closer she can see between the trees that the so-called hut is an old wood structure, actually quite big, built into the side of the cliff.

Mr Quah catches up to her.

"This is it," he says.

"What is 'it' exactly?" Sophie asks. "This building doesn't resemble a temple. I don't think many people would come here. Let's knock on the door and find out."

Sophie is about to take a step forward.

Mr Quah steps forward and says, "Wait. I'll go first."

He takes a brave breath.

"There won't be anything bad. This is just a house," Sophie says to reassure him.

Mr Quah says, "Who would live here?"

He has a point.

They cautiously approach the building together.

Mr Quah knocks and yells in Chinese, "Sorry to bother you but we are tourists, somewhat lost, please help!"

The door opens and an old man lets them inside.

"Thank you very much," Sophie says in English, hoping he understands.

She briefly studies him as she walks inside. He is very short and very frail.

Will he be able to help us?

"Sit by the fire," he says in English, which is a great relief to Sophie.

The old man then rushes out of the room.

"I am hot from walking even though the air is very cold outside," Sophie tells Mr Quah.

"Me too, but the place is cosy," he replies as he takes his coat off.

Sophie inspects around the house. Timber beams make up the walls and ceiling. Maybe the old man made the structure himself, when he was younger.

At that moment the old man returns to the room with cups of water for Sophie and Mr Quah.

"I don't get many visitors anymore," the old man explains, "since they flooded the village. Before that I was the 'wise man' so to speak. People would come to me almost daily to talk. Are you here to talk? You don't look like tourists. Is something troubling you two?"

Sophie realises she is frowning and tries to relax, pretending to be at peace with the world.

Mr Quah decides to speak up.

"We are actually here to see you. A monk advised us of this mountain. We really do need help."

Mr Quah knows he is not making much sense but how can he explain to this old man why he and Sophie have travelled here to talk with him.

"Do tell me what is bothering you both," the old man says as he shifts in his chair, ready to listen and offer advice.

"We want to know about a lady who lived long ago," Sophie says.

"I've met many people over the years," the old man tells her.

"You might not have met this woman," Mr Quah says.

Sophie blurts out, "Lan Zhu-Ku."

She can't hold back any longer. She wants answers.

"Let me search my memory," the old man says. "I do recollect the name. She was troubled. Her husband was not faithful."

"Yes, we read about that too," Mr Quah says.

He worries now that this old man can't offer any more help than the books.

"She was very sad about being betrayed," the old man recalls. "My wife tried talking to her but she ran away from town fearing everybody would laugh at her. She was ashamed at being lied to. Back then the townspeople did not have much sympathy. She was in the wrong according to them."

"And she hid in the mountains so the townspeople would not punish her for giving birth out of wedlock now that she has left her husband," Sophie says, reciting what she remembers from the book.

"There was no child," the old man says.

Mr Quah turns to Sophie and says, "We've been after the wrong person this whole time."

"Your brain needs to be enlightened," the old man says to Mr Quah.

Sophie says, "We read in some very old books that Lan had a child. The child was raised with retribution installed in its mind. When that child grew up and had a child of its own the process was repeated. This happened for a number of generations so the instinct of the child is revenge. Now Miss Serizawa, who we know, is the latest descendent of Lan. Or so we thought."

"Humans instinctively make things easier for themselves," the old man tells them. "If they don't understand something they either ignore whatever they have an issue with or modify the facts until the information makes sense to them. Humans also like sharing thoughts and don't want to come across as foolish so they tell a relative or friend this new fact that they have learnt. Of course they tell the modified version.

Over the years the facts become a fictional story. Over the years the fictional story becomes an unsolvable myth. The story you have read is very old. But the facts are older. They have changed, been modified and turned into a story. Quite different to what happened thousands of years ago. Let me tell you some facts."

The old man gets comfortable in his chair. Sophie, now at room temperature, finally feels warm enough to take off her jacket. Mr Quah takes a sip of water, ready to learn from this wise old man.

"During 420BCE in the province of Chang'an," he begins, "a young girl's father is to become the ruler now that her grandfather has died. But her father's younger brother kills him so that he can be the new ruler. The townspeople are too scared to revolt. When the young girl learns who murdered her father she cries for seven years and her only thoughts are that her uncle gets harmed somehow. After the seven years is over her uncle is found dead in his room. Now the girl's family becomes the new rulers. And rightly so. The townspeople may suspect the girl was involved but are too happy that the evil uncle is dead.

The young lady, now a princess, uses all her powers to do good by helping struggling farmers and teaching children.

She spends all her life helping others.

Four years after her death she is rewarded for her kindness and is granted goddess stature. She vows to continue her good will and is named Goddess of Fairness and Equality."

Sophie and Mr Quah have been sitting quietly listening to every word.

This will link with Miss Serizawa soon, Mr Quah tells himself.

Sophie is telling herself the same thing.

"Now, in 108BCE," the old man starts up again, "a farmer's daughter is working hard in their field. Right now is harvest time and she wants to help her dad who is ill in bed. Emperor Ji Tuo is passing through the farm village on his way to his palace. Townspeople gather by the roadside to wave. Off to his left he sees from his carriage there is a lone farmer working away. No one else in the town seems to be working so he asks his servants to stop. As he approaches the field he sees the farmer is a young lady. She is working so hard that she doesn't notice him.

"Why are you working so hard today?" he calls to the young lady as he walks closer.

She stands nervously and replies, "My dad is sick in bed. He needs this field harvested today so we can take the grain to market in the next province to sell tomorrow."

"What is your name?" he asks.

"Lan Zhu-Ku," she replies.

She knows this man is the Emperor and wonders why he would talk to her.

"Can I help you Lan?" he asks.

"I couldn't ask you to help me," Lan says, staring at her feet.

She is too shy to raise her eyes up to the Emperor.

"You didn't ask. I want to help," he says and begins to harvest.

They work away, not talking, until the field is harvested. By the end his robes are very dirty and Lan is worried he will be mad.

"Your clothes," she says, feeling terrible.

He laughs it off, "I have enjoyed helping you."

"Thank you very much," Lan says.

"I must get going. I've imposed too much. Good luck at market," he says and quickly walks away.

Off he goes in his carriage with his servants. Lan believes she will never see him again.

One week later Lan has a messenger come to her door. He leaves her a note.

"Dad," she calls out, "I have a letter from Emperor Ji Tuo."

She walks into his room and shows her father.

"He has invited me to dinner at the palace tonight. I'm scared."

Her father looks proudly at his daughter and says, "Go. Visiting the palace will be fun for you."

He knows this is a once in a lifetime opportunity. He, just like his parents before him, has worked hard all his life, struggling with backbreaking farm work.

"If a good offer comes along you must jump at the chance," he explains.

Lan and the Emperor meet on many occasions over the next weeks. To the shock of the townspeople, for she is a mere peasant, one evening he asks Lan to marry him.

She is in love and says yes. They live happily for five years. Their lives are perfect.

Through no fault of hers, for she does nothing wrong, Tuo seduces other women. Lan finds out and her life crumbles. His infidelity has been happening for years. Lan is so embarrassed by him. So embarrassed that everyone seems to have known except her. She is laughed at by the townspeople for they trust she must not have been a good enough wife. She runs away.

The Goddess of Fairness and Equality finds Lan one day who has been crying for seven years. The Goddess decides to help Lan. She grants Lan Zhu-Ku immortality if Lan agrees to help one thousand women who are wronged by their loved ones. After she helps one thousand women she

will become mortal again and live out the
rest of her years, knowing she has helped
many women who experienced the same
as she experienced with Tuo.

Lan Zhu-Ku agrees and promises she
will do all she can to help one thousand
women who are wronged. Her anger has
risen dramatically over the seven years she
has been hiding in the mountains. Now
she can take on this new role and live a
new life.

Lan Zhu-Ku's first act as an immortal,
in keeping her promise to her Goddess, is
as follows:

Lan dresses up as a man. She walks
down the mountain to her old hometown
posing as a beggar. She stalks Emperor Ji
Tuo and finds out he has remarried. Lan
comes up with a plan. She finds a nice
room to rent and dresses up as a beautiful
woman, disguising herself so the Emperor
will not recognise that she is his old wife.
The next day she follows the Emperor to
a shopping district. She bumps into him
on purpose and apologises. He doesn't
recognise her through the disguise but is
attracted instantly. Lan invites him back

to her room that evening. He agrees to meet her after the sun has set. The next day Emperor Ji Tuo is found with his head sliced clean off. He will never seduce again. Lan Zhu-Ku watches the townspeople panic from her hideout in the mountains. Nine hundred and ninety nine to go."

The old man finishes talking.

Mr Quah and Sophie look at each other. They have learnt a lot in a very short amount of time.

"How do you know all this? Why should we believe you and not the books?" Mr Quah asks.

"Are you a god?" Sophie asks the old man.

He shakes his head from side to side and says, "I'm not a god. The gods don't like me."

"I know what you mean, they don't like me either. I never have any good luck," Mr Quah says.

The humour is lost on the old man and he continues talking.

"They have punished me. Sentenced me to endless life. I want to die but they won't let me. Not until I have served my time."

Mr Quah has a sudden feeling that he knows what the man is on about.

"I wanted to be immortal when I was a child," he says.

Sophie turns to Mr Quah. She will catch on soon.

"Many people out there wish they could live longer," the old man says. "They feel one normal life isn't enough time to accomplish their goals. When death comes near they are fearful and don't want to leave their loved ones. Would two or three lifetimes be better for them? When does one go from 'Please let me live longer' to 'Please let me die'. Personally I have witnessed my children grow up and die. I've witnessed my grand children grow old and die. And their children and their children. To watch someone be born, live and die like they are specks of dust is torture. I don't even know if I have any family out there anymore. My brain is starting to shut down. I have trouble remembering short-term things. I start doing something and halfway though I wonder why I'm standing in a certain place in the room. Physically I feel good. I have slowed down everything I do, as I get tired easily, but this is not too big a problem. Living to one hundred may sound great. Living to four hundred might appeal to some. You will have more of an opportunity to be able to achieve all of your goals but eventually you realise living forever is a curse and all you want is to be mortal again. I'm over two thousand years old. I've come to the point where I can see that nothing matters. Anything you or I do will not matter in time. The world doesn't care. The planets and suns and stars watch, just like I do. They have seen it all before.

Immortality is a curse but treated right, you can become very wise. You will learn every mystery in the universe and become very relaxed with any event which may arise. If you don't seek immortality simply being alive can easily make you insane and you crumble, begging the gods to kill you. That happened to me five hundred years ago. Yet I'm still here. Living a short life is the best thing that can happen to you. You have enough time to dream, fall in love, eat good food and have offspring. Enjoy every second."

Sophie and Mr Quah don't know what to say.

Sophie comes up with something.

"You didn't want to be immortal?" she asks.

"No. I angered the gods and this is how they punished me," he explains.

The old man lifts his eyes to the ceiling but both Mr Quah and Sophie know he is looking far beyond. He is miles away, in a dark place, trying to find the gods that have put this curse on him.

"We think we know where Lan is now. She goes under the name of Miss Serizawa," Mr Quah says, changing the subject.

The old man seems surprised.

"I thought she would have got to her thousand quite quickly. She seemed to enjoy her 'job' when I knew of her."

"She has recruited two others to help her so she isn't actually doing the 'job' anymore but keeps on living. She has probably had many help her over the years," Sophie explains, piecing everything together in her mind.

"We need to stop her. What Miss Serizawa is doing is against the law," Mr Quah says.

The old man stands up as he gets an idea. He walks to a bookshelf.

"I am immortal because of a curse. Living forever is my punishment. All I can do is sit and wait for the gods to let me die. Wait for my punishment to be over. My life is in their hands. There are other ways to become immortal. Before phoenices became extinct Emperors who owned one would use a pin to draw a phial of blood from the phoenix's chest. He could only extract blood once per bird but drinking the blood would make the Emperor live an extra few years. They could also give some of the blood to heal injured warriors and ninjas. Drinking the phoenix blood didn't protect the army from dying from normal means, but did heal injuries and made the person feel stronger. Emperors were too ignorant to realise phoenix numbers were dropping until it was too late and the bird became extinct. Now, Lan Zhu-Ku was granted immortality by the gods who were helping her. Living forever isn't a curse to her. Eternal life is a reward for her suffering when she was younger. Lan wants to stay immortal for as long as she can. She enjoys her task. She doesn't care about Earthly morals and laws. The gods might, but changing their minds now is too late as they made an agreement. They said she is to help one thousand women who are hurt by their loved ones. They didn't know Lan would use her built up rage to go killing men."

"How do we stop her?" Sophie asks, watching the old man flick through a pile of scrolls.

Mr Quah adds, "If we arrest her she will start back up again when released."

"She was granted immortality as a reward," the old man says. "She took a bite of the peach. Her life ends when the deal is over and the deal is to help one thousand women. Who knows how many she's helped so far. Who knows how many women she's had helping her over the years. The reward needs to be taken away from her."

The old man continues flicking through the scrolls, scanning the paper for any information which may help.

"How? Should we kill her?" Sophie asks.

"That will kill the body who you call Miss Serizawa," the old man tells her, "but the job won't be finished so the spirit of Lan will be in limbo which is dangerous because she may find a way to come back in a different body at some point in the next million years. You need to kill her spirit. Stop the spirit thinking it has to help women. Spirits are very powerful but they can be broken. Send the spirit to the afterlife and you will never have a problem again."

"How do we stop the spirit?" Mr Quah asks.

"If you can find a phoenix and give the blood to Miss Serizawa somehow, this may reverse the immortal process. Hopefully stopping her heart and sending the spirit off forever," the old man refers to the scroll he has found.

Sophie knows these scrolls must be ancient and may very much help them, but they are out of date by a few hundred years.

She says, "Well phoenices have been extinct for over a thousand years so there goes that idea."

"You could try finding an Emperor who used to use phoenix blood," the old man suggests. "Their DNA will have remains of the bird blood."

"There won't be any Emperors alive anymore since the birds died out," Mr Quah points out. "What about your DNA?"

Mr Quah wonders how this old man knows about DNA, but then he has plenty of time to keep up on the events of the rapidly changing world.

"I was forced to be immortal. I didn't choose eternal life. Lan wants to live forever so I recommend finding DNA of a willing immortal. I know of an Emperor buried a few provinces away. Emperor Qian. He lived to nearly one thousand years old. Unfortunately he went quite insane after seeing his grandchildren born and then die of old age right before his eyes."

"That's the price you pay," Sophie says.

"Being immortal never seems a good idea," Mr Quah adds.

"So this Emperor Qian could help us?" Sophie asks the old man.

"He lived to one thousand because, like Miss Serizawa, he wanted to. If I remember correctly, Emperor Qian actually stopped taking phoenix blood by choice, not because they died out. He wanted to be normal again. Perhaps if you dig up Emperor Qian's remains, grind up one of his bones into a powder and feed this to Miss Serizawa the DNA of Emperor Qian will be absorbed into her blood stream. The desire of Emperor Qian to return to mortality may also pass into Miss Serizawa and her body will be so shocked the evil spirit may not be able to cope. Hopefully this will cause her to die a natural death and the evil spirit will be sent off to the afterlife where it will have to deal with the gods."

"I guess that's what we have to do," Sophie says to Mr Quah.

All three rise with the unspoken understanding that the answer is now before them.

"Thank you for coming to see me," the old man says to them both.

Mr Quah and Sophie express their gratitude to the old man for taking the time to talk with them. He has helped them immensely.

"Coming here has been very beneficial," Mr Quah says.

"Don't thank me," the old man says as he shows them out. "Having you as company was nice. I just hope my advice will be useful. Personally, I have tried a few techniques to become mortal once more, yet I am still here. So I wish you the best of luck."

Back in Japan, Alana finds herself dozing beside the radio. She wakes as yet another news report is sent out over the city, listened to by anxious citizens wondering if walking the streets while the moon shines is yet safe.

"*. . . nobody was in the office at the time of the explosion, although some workers in neighbouring offices were injured in the blast which is thought to have been small but very intense. A number of pedestrians were struck by falling debris but as far as we have heard all are recovering well. The Chief of the Metropolitan Police Department is still shocked at what he saw and how close he came to being in his office when the parcel bomb went off. He has vowed to bring those responsible to justice.*

Some members of the public are wondering if this will ever happen. There is growing anger in the community as to why these women are still at large. The government's offer of a reward for any information from the public which leads to an arrest has so far yielded no results. What will it take to end this nightmare? If there is proof that this latest incident was the work of the four little maids, more unnecessary fuel will be added to the already out-of-control fire as doubt surrounding power of the authorities' increases . . . ."

Chapter Fourteen

"**P**oor man," Sophie says to Mr Quah as they follow the waterway back down the mountain.

"Why feel sorry for him? He is serving his punishment," Mr Quah points out. "We don't know what he did to the gods to make them so mad. Eventually they will lift the curse and let him die."

After a short silence to consider everything that has happened, Sophie comes up with a thought.

"Miss Serizawa is training Azuna and Fusako. Azuna and Fusako may have been made immortal by Miss Serizawa as a prize for helping her.

"Kayami will possibly be added to the group and you may be invited too once you help Miss Serizawa with something big," Mr Quah says.

"Which I don't plan to do," Sophie says firmly.

"Unfortunately I think you will have to prove yourself at some stage," Mr Quah says.

Sophie doesn't like the sound of that.

"Great," she says under her breath.

After descending further down the mountain slope Sophie has another thought.

"I wonder," she says, "if we ever manage to stop Miss Serizawa, or kill her off, will the immortality that is lifted from her be lifted from Azuna and Fusako too or will they pick up from where Miss Serizawa has stopped?"

"We'll find out."

At the bottom of the mountain they hop back into the boat. Mr Quah begins to paddle.

The boat ride takes what seems like only seconds. Sophie and Mr Quah talk the whole time. Each is very excited.

"We learnt so much from the old man and now have a way we can try to stop Miss Serizawa," Sophie says.

"I think we are still a fair way off from resolving this, but once we sort out the finer details of our plan I am confident things will work in our favour," Mr Quah says.

He doesn't even notice his burning arm muscles from rowing.

Back at the side of the lake Mr Quah ties the boat to the small rickety jetty and runs to Sophie who is sitting in the rental car checking the street directory.

"The old man said Emperor Qian is buried in a temple further east of here," Mr Quah says while Sophie searches for the town in the directory.

"Here it is!" Sophie says excitedly. "The temple is only half an hours drive in the direction of the city."

Mr Quah goes to start the car but again, Sophie stops him.

"We can't just go to a temple and start digging up the main attraction," she points out. "What if we find a relative of his that's recently died and dig up their bones. Their DNA might have a trace of the phoenix blood."

"I don't want to take that risk," Mr Quah states. "We should at least check out the temple's security."

"Let's go," Sophie agrees.

Nearly an hour later, Sophie and Mr Quah are out the front of a small shrine surrounded by a botanic garden. While they eat lunch at a food stall they survey the area. There doesn't seem to be any security. There doesn't seem to be any public around either.

"Are we at the right place?" Sophie says.

Mr Quah asks, "Where do we pay? I'm a bit confused."

"Maybe this temple has to be free to attract visitors, but from the lack of patrons that doesn't seem to have worked," Sophie says.

Not long after people come out of the shrine to prove her wrong.

As this group wanders off happily taking in their surroundings a new group of people come along to take their place inside. Sophie guesses that the normal visitor here will be a student doing an assignment on the Emperor inside or they are a tourist on a budget and don't want to pay to tour one of the bigger temples.

"Try to see if there are any security cameras," Mr Quah says to Sophie as they walk inside to blend in with the group.

Sophie can't see any cameras but clearly sees the two security officers.

Mr Quah and Sophie hang to the walls watching the tourists.

Sophie starts looking at plaques on the wall next to her and reads the English translations. She comes across an interesting paragraph: *'Emperor Qian now spends his time listening to the visitors all day who wonder to each other whether the myth that he lived to 1000 years old is true or not.'*

Sophie shows Mr Quah the plaque and he reads the inscription.

Mr Quah says, "Having the skeleton right there in the casket is a shame. So close yet so far."

"Let's quickly open the lid, you hold back the guards while I grab one of the Emperor's bones and we'll run back to the car," Sophie suggests, knowing the idea is ridiculous.

"Or we could ask them for a bone as a souvenir," Mr Quah says.

They walk out of the shrine and wander along a garden path. Both are glum.

"So we'll break in then?" Sophie asks.

Mr Quah says, "I'll have to."

He pauses for a minute.

"You go back home," he tells Sophie. "Your daughter needs you there."

They continue strolling the grounds.

"What are you going to do? The airline won't let you change your ticket again," Sophie says.

"I'll buy a new one and fly out tomorrow. I'll get the first plane back as soon as I can get to the airport."

"You're going to break into the temple alone?" Sophie asks.

"That's the best idea we have. Actually there aren't many other options for us. I'll break in after midnight and open the casket."

He can't wait to get his hands dirty.

"I want to help," Sophie says.

"No," Mr Quah says firmly. "If we get caught then this has all been a waste of time. And your daughter will be in danger while we sit here in jail."

Sophie knows he is right.

Mr Quah continues, "Go home. At least if I get caught you still have plan B."

"Which is?" Sophie says, looking at Mr Quah for an answer.

"I'm not sure."

PART THREE

Chapter Fifteen

Sophie slowly walks along a dark road in her make-up and kimono. The neighbouring houses are all very quiet. Occasionally she can see glows from the houses and Sophie guesses most people are sleeping. The occupants are too afraid to venture out unnecessarily in these dangerous times. A light fog in the air makes the glow from the lights seem even more eerie.

No cars are in earshot as Sophie crosses the road. She stops at a gate. Before crossing the threshold she gazes around behind her. She can't see any sign of life through the darkness. From what she can tell, no one is following. Sophie opens the gate as quietly as she can. Every little metallic scrape sounds deafening. Her shallow breathing sounds deafening. She is sure she has woken the whole street.

Sophie holds her breath and goes through the gate, listening for human life. Nothing. Through the gate she resumes breathing, as there been no exclamations of her presence. She takes in her new location. The blackness makes seeing her surroundings very difficult but as far as she can tell apartments rise up either side of her.

Where is Azuna?

Sophie walks down the path. One apartment should be Kayami's, if she's in the right alleyway. Miss Serizawa, Azuna, Fusako and Kayami should be around here somewhere. Sophie is to meet them and kill Kayami's husband.

Days earlier . . .

By the time Sophie arrives back at her street from the airport she can't see out of the taxi's windows as the night sky is pitch black. From what she can hear, as she climbs out of the car, nobody is awake in her neighbourhood. She is very glad to be home and she hurries inside. She is a new woman after the trip to China.

Sophie rushes to her daughter's room.

"Mum?" Alana asks after Sophie gently wakes her daughter.

Sophie replies, "I'm home. I missed you. Are you well? Is everything safe?"

She kisses her daughter on the forehead and holds Alana's arms as she talks.

"Yes, don't worry. I am fine. Nobody came knocking."

"I'm sorry I was gone for so long. Did I miss anything?" Sophie asks.

"No, the police car has been outside the whole time," Alana explains. "The latest news report now though is that a group of rich businessmen have decided to offer the four women millions of dollars in exchange for ending their evil ways. The government says the offer is very irresponsible but the public are all for the idea since the government's reward for information was not successful."

"Somehow I don't think money will stop them but this shows that a handful of people are trying to come up with a way to make the women cease their actions. They just don't realise what they are dealing with," Sophie adds.

Sophie talks briefly with her daughter about recent events. Alana listens carefully and is astounded. She can't believe what happened in China. Sophie then gets ready for bed. Seconds after climbing into bed she falls asleep from pure exhaustion.

Meanwhile . . .

Armed with a pillowcase, a pocket full of gloves and a bobby pin he found at a bus stop earlier, Mr Quah tiptoes through the grounds of the temple. He had caught a train which dropped him at a station nearby and then walked the remaining few blocks, careful to not be seen. He arrived at the gardens which houses the temple safely, at just after one in the morning.

The surrounds are very quiet. There is not a soul to be seen. Mr Quah walks through the gardens and finally locates the temple. He walks around to the back. He finds a wooden door along the back wall. Mr Quah decides this is going to be his point of entry. The first thing to do is put on gloves before touching anything.

Of course this door is bolted shut with an old padlock. Mr Quah spends ten minutes trying to pick the lock. After being unsuccessful he kicks the padlock which busts open.

Mr Quah makes his way quietly, feeling his way with his hands, to the room with the casket containing the once immortal Emperor Qian.

Mr Quah is about to attempt to lift the casket lid when a security guard walks into the room.

"What do you think you're doing!"

The security guard yells at Mr Quah and shines his torch into Mr Quah's eyes.

Mr Quah jumps.

"I'm a policeman from Japan," Mr Quah says.

He quickly shows the guard his identification.

"What are you doing here?" the security guard asks as he relaxes a bit but is still wary of the intruder.

"I need a bone of a former immortal Emperor," Mr Quah explains. "There is an evil woman where I live. She has killed hundreds of men over hundreds of years. A bone crushed up can apparently stop her. Please let me take one."

Saying all this as believably as he can, Mr Quah can't help but realise how absurd the words must sound. He fears he is going to be thrown out and told never to return.

The security guard says, "Your story sounds odd but I find myself guarding a temple which holds the bones of Emperor Qian, rumoured to be immortal, six hours a night. Why shouldn't I believe you?"

Mr Quah is glad to hear this response.

"You'll turn the other way while I do this?" Mr Quah asks anxiously.

"No, I'll help you. I don't want to get blamed so we will make the room appear exactly how it was. Deal?"

Mr Quah knows this is his best offer.

"Deal," he says to the security guard. "Here are some gloves."

The security guard helps Mr Quah open the casket. They carefully place the heavy stone lid on the ground. Mr Quah takes another of his brave breaths, ready to peer over the side of the open casket.

As Mr Quah expects, the bones aren't laid out neatly. A thousand year old skeleton doesn't hold together like skeletons in a science lab. No, the bones in the casket in front of Mr Quah are all over the place. The skull is at one end of the casket on its side. The legs are at the other end nearly all wasted down to nothing. They look too brittle to touch. The rib cage has collapsed. Maybe the casket has been transported from time to time, knocked about, from museum to museum.

'Emperor Qian certainly has had a rough life, or rather death,' Mr Quah says to himself, 'until you finally had a temple built for you where you now reside in peace. Sorry about this.'

Regardless of all of this Mr Quah needs bones. Unless an archaeologist or University student has opened the casket and taken note or sketched the layout of the skeleton, Mr Quah feels lucky. He doubts any one will notice two missing bones among this mess. He reaches in . . . .

The security guard helps Mr Quah carefully lift and replace the casket lid, sliding the stone slab back into the original position, so nobody will be able to tell the casket has been tampered with.

Mr Quah remembers a minor detail.

"I broke the lock getting in here," he tells the security guard.

The security guard thinks for a moment.

"There is an old garden shed where the grounds keepers store their tools. I'll swap the locks. They will believe the garden shed has been broken into rather than the temple."

As they walk out Mr Quah thanks the security guard.

"Don't thank me," he says. "Good luck with everything. I wish I could know how you go."

Mr Quah leaves from the back door while the security guard examines the broken lock.

In the black of night, Mr Quah eventually finds his way out of the temple's labyrinth of botanic gardens and walks along the main road. He keeps his eyes out for a passing taxi as he walks towards the city. He will not risk catching a train where anyone could stop him and talk to him and question him.

Mr Quah feels quite happy. He has the rib bones wrapped up in the pillowcase which is tucked into his shirt. All he has to do now is get back to his hotel room, tape the ribs to his chest and get to the airport by sunrise.

Soon he will be back in Japan crushing the ribs and feeding them to an immortal woman.

Finally a taxi drives by which Mr Quah waves down. He is not interested in walking anymore. He can doze until the taxi stops at his hotel.

At the end of a drinking session inside one of the city's packed karaoke bars a couple help each other walk hand in hand towards the exit. This is a regular night out for these two lovebirds. One of the many common interests that they share. They attend architect classes together and spend endless nights lying on the grass looking up at the stars talking about their dream of travelling the globe to join in on the latest architecture movement which incorporates modern art and design with flowing structures and sculptures. Gone is the rigidity of a cold closed off world. Borders are now being opened on so many levels.

A small stumble along the lake's paved shore will take these inseparable souls to their converted warehouse of an apartment. The age of the population around these streets averages below twenty-five. 'Possibilities are endless' is the communal belief.

At this time of night the distant hum of the city is a constant entity which is so normal the noise goes unnoticed. The sound of a speedboat puttering along at a slow rate of knots, however, is unusual. Although the senses of the loving couple are dulled from all the sake, the noise manages to penetrate their ears. Perhaps the speedboat is returning from a day trip along the coast. Nothing out of the ordinary with that notion.

The boat begins to speed up. This does seem out of the ordinary. There are many boats moored out on the lake here and to the intoxicated couple, speeding along in the dark does not seem wise.

They stop to watch.

"Perhaps the throttle is jammed," says the man. "This will surely end in tears."

"The boat seems to be steering alright," the young woman says.

Again the speed is increased as the boat turns straight for a large yacht moored on the bay.

"Did someone just slide off the speedboat into the water?" the man asks.

"I didn't notice," the woman replies.

The couple brace themselves for the impact, stiffening up as if they themselves are on the boat and about to crash.

Eventually the inevitable happens. The starboards bow of the speedboat impacts with the luxury cruiser with tremendous force. From what they can see, a huge hole is torn abeam to port side of the pride and joy of a soon to be very upset owner.

"Hopefully nobody is onboard the yacht," the woman says.

Our lovebirds race, as much as they can race, to their apartment to call the authorities. Both are too drunk to stay up and watch all the excitement. They will surely hear all about the crash in the morning.

Chapter Sixteen

Sophie wakes up with a jolt. She panics, wondering where she is. Am I still in China? Where is Mr Quah?

But soon Sophie remembers that she made the trip safely home. Through blurry eyes she sees her alarm clock tick over to thirty-eight minutes past four in the morning. She suddenly becomes wide-awake as she realises Mr Quah would have broken into the temple by now. Did he get the bones? He must be out. Did he get seen? Is he waiting safely at Beijing airport for the first flight out?

Sophie doesn't fall back to sleep. She lies there thinking until morning.

Meanwhile . . .

Mr Quah's taxi crashes off the road. Mr Quah is shocked by the sudden stop. He lifts his head to a sight of the driver passed out hunched over the steering wheel with blood trickling from his ear, which is never a good sign. Mr Quah turns to find the cause of the crash. A car up the street has pulled over and two men are getting out.

Did they hit the taxi off the road? Who are they? Police?

Mr Quah assumes they are after him for taking the ribs. He doesn't want to have to explain the story to them. They won't believe him. Even if they do believe what he tells them he won't get to his flight in time.

Mr Quah opens the furthest taxi door away from the police and runs. He doesn't look back. He has no idea if they are chasing him or not. He runs down alleyways, across streets, down hills, he keeps running and running. Eventually he checks over his shoulder. Nobody seems to be there. Mr Quah stops running. He listens. There are no sounds of approaching sirens or footsteps. When he catches his breath he carefully walks, like a frightened cat, the remaining four blocks to his hotel.

The lobby is empty of guests which is no surprise. The receptionist looks up briefly but is more interested in whatever he is reading. Mr Quah walks up to the counter.

"Good evening, Sir," the receptionist says, standing to attention.

"Has my ticket come through yet?" Mr Quah asks.

The receptionist checks the hotel email account.

"Yes," he says, "your flight details have been sent to us. I'll print the ticket for you."

The receptionist walks around the corner and comes back with Mr Quah's new plane ticket.

"Thank you," Mr Quah tells him.

As Mr Quah walks away the receptionist goes back to his reading.

Mr Quah feels safe once he is alone in the elevator. He dreams of washing up. Shaving. Perhaps even having an hour's nap before the dawn flight.

After washing up with warm water, which feels unbelievable, Mr Quah is fifty percent better. He really needs that sleep. As he walks around the main room bed, ready to lie down, he notices out of the bedroom window a car parking down on street level. Mr Quah watches as two people get out. They rush towards the hotel entrance before going out of view. Mr Quah knows the callers have come to pay him a visit so he pockets his wallet and tucks the ribs into his shirt. He is ready for a quick escape. He exits his room and sees that the elevator numbers are lighting up one by one as his visitors ascend. Mr Quah shuts his room door giving the illusion that he is still inside, while he walks rapidly to the fire exit.

Halfway down the fire exit stairs Mr Quah realises someone is walking up. Surely they would have heard his descending footsteps, as he hadn't been going quietly. He ducks out one of the floor doors and waits.

The pursuer opens the floor door and Mr Quah attacks. The man gets knocked to the ground. Mr Quah falls too while arms and legs fly everywhere. Just as the pursuer seems to be winning Mr Quah elbows him in the jaw as hard as he can. This does the job. Mr Quah gets up and runs back into the fire exit and doesn't stop running until he is down in the lobby. The receptionist is dead behind the counter. These aren't police.

The men's car is idling by the roadside. The same car that had ran Mr Quah's taxi off the road earlier in the night. Mr Quah suspects they wanted a quick getaway after they had dealt with him so he decides to take advantage of this. He gets into the car and, as damaged as the front panels are, Mr Quah drives off. He is several blocks away before one of the men runs outside of the hotel entrance scratching his head, his partner upstairs trying to climb to his feet.

Mr Quah drives straight for the airport. There he will be able to have a small sleep at the departure gate. That's all he cares about now.

He drives through the city and out the other side towards the airport and during the drive he has a moment to check himself. He knows he put the plane ticket in his wallet. He pats his pants pocket and feels the wallet safe inside. The ribs were wrapped in the pillowcase. He feels his stomach. The pillowcase is safely tucked into his shirt. Mr Quah wishes he could have hid the bones better.

His plane flight is scheduled to depart in a couple of hours so Mr Quah is hoping to have time to visit the toilets and adjust the pillowcase of ribs. Perhaps he can call into a newsagent and buy some tape.

Up ahead on the road Mr Quah sees flashing lights. If they were orange the lights would indicate road works and that would not be a problem. There may be delays but there won't be any reason to panic.

As Mr Quah drives closer he can make out that they are the blue and red lights of the Chinese police, different to the red lights of Japanese police that he is accustomed to. Mr Quah has cause for panic. This is likely to be a roadblock. They are likely to be after Mr Quah.

Calmly to avoid suspicion, he indicates and turns on to a side road. He parks at a supermarket and wonders how guilty he just looked but luckily the flashing lights remain unmoved which means that he was not noticed.

The two men before were obviously not police but Mr Quah suspects the body of the dead receptionist has been discovered and now the police must be on high alert. A murderer is on the loose. They've been told to erect roadblocks.

Now what? Will they be patrolling the airports, ports and train stations? Will they be checking every passenger on outgoing flights?

Mr Quah leaves the car he borrowed and walks into the supermarket with his backpack. Surprisingly there are actually people shopping at four in the morning in this centre so he is thankful that he won't be looked at twice. Mr Quah walks casually to the public toilets. Twenty minutes later an old man, same height and weight, and same backpack, walks out. Surely nobody has realised that this is the same person. Now he has to get to the departure gate.

Mr Quah walks out on to the street and looks down the road towards the flashing lights. He comes up with a plan. The airport entrance is a few minutes drive down the road beyond the flashing lights but just a few hundred metres away there looks to be a service entrance. Mr Quah soon hails a passing taxi and in no time at all gets out again and is standing by the service entrance gates. The taxi drives away. Mr Quah begins to walk through the gate.

An impatient voice calls out, "Sir, you can't come through here."

An airport security guard walks over to Mr Quah.

"Isn't this the airport entrance?" Mr Quah asks, putting on a confused face and beginning to sound panicked.

"No, this is for workers only. Service vehicles and deliveries," the security guard informs Mr Quah.

"Oh, my taxi has driven off," Mr Quah says and stares off down the long road towards the flashing lights.

The security guard watches the taxi driving away.

Mr Quah asks, "Can I come through here? I'm an old man. My plane takes off in half an hour."

The security guard feels sorry for the bewildered man. He lets Mr Quah through.

"I'll have someone meet you down that hall there," the security guard explains and points. "They will take you to the departure gate."

Mr Quah smiles and says, "Sorry for the bungle. Thank you, kind sir."

Mr Quah tries not to look too happy. The security guard walks to his booth to make the phone call as Mr Quah walks into the hallway. The plan has worked.

Minutes later, Mr Quah is escorted right to his gate and is the first person to board while onlookers feel sorry for the frail old man.

After all the other passengers have boarded the flight, which to Mr Quah seems to have taken forever, the plane begins to taxi to the runway. Mr Quah surveys the terminal. Everything seems calm. No flashing police lights are to be seen. No men are waving frantically to get the attention of the pilot. Mr Quah feels confident as the plane takes off into the sky.

As Mr Quah falls asleep, Sophie is arriving at the lake having to endure Tai Chi with her "friends".

"Good morning, Kayami," she says.

"Are you feeling better, Sophie?" Miss Serizawa asks.

"A little, I am still taking tablets," Sophie replies.

"That's no good," Azuna says.

"At least I'm on the mend," Sophie tells them.

She now has to act all happy and healthy. During Tai Chi of course all her thoughts were on Mr Quah and Miss Serizawa. Miss Serizawa goes about her daily life as if nothing is wrong. Nobody would suspect her of any wrongdoing. Sophie feels horrible being so close to Miss Serizawa, less than two metres from this old woman who has personally killed who knows how many men. Sophie can't wait until this nightmare is all over. She and Mr Quah will rid the world of this woman. Sophie is very pleased when Tai Chi is over for the day.

Chapter Seventeen

Mr Quah wakes up with a jolt. The plane has started to descend as they approach Japan and Mr Quah's ears must have popped.

He feels better after the sleep but panics as he realises there may be waiting policemen wanting to escort him off the plane. Will they go to those measures for a little theft? He stole some bones. Maybe a small fine might be issued but he doubts his thievery will be an international incident.

'But then there's the dead receptionist,' Mr Quah says to himself.

He stands and goes to the bathroom to check his disguise.

In the bathroom Mr Quah quickly touches up his hair and face and checks his extra ribs before the seatbelt lights come on and he has to sit back in his seat.

Minutes later the plane lands smoothly and taxis to the terminal while Mr Quah scans the tarmac. As in China no flashing police car lights are to be seen in this part of the world either. Mr Quah tries to scan the terminal windows but he can't see through the tinted glass. Once off the plane and walking through the terminal with the other passengers to collect their luggage Mr Quah relaxes. There are no police waiting to arrest him, disguised or not, so he walks outside to catch a taxi to safety and hopes to put this whole trip behind him.

Sophie is being driven to a client's apartment by Mr Nguyen. They have stopped at a red light. Earlier in the morning Mr Nguyen called Sophie to tell her an apartment needs cleaning and arranged to pick Sophie up. She feels ill. All she can think about is whether Mr Quah has made his journey back to Japan safely or if he is in trouble, or jail, in China.

As the van drives on to the apartment Sophie wonders about the other people driving around. They have their routines, their worries, their loved ones and their happy memories. They earn money to eat and buy nice things and they sleep comfortably and happily in their warm beds. They have unrealistic goals and big dreams. They have no idea about the wide world around them. So much is going on out there that nobody realises. Sophie had no idea about the world until recently. She will never be the same again. Never close down and be self-absorbed like most others. Any person could walk past Miss Serizawa in a supermarket believing she is just another elderly citizen. Harmless. Little do they know.

Mr Nguyen parks the van and Sophie hops out.

"Thank you," she says.

"See you one hour," he says loudly as he drives off.

Sophie knocks at the door.

A familiar voice calls out, "Come in."

Sophie walks through the apartment door with all her cleaning products under her arms. Her eyes light up. Standing inside is Mr Quah, holding a briefcase.

Sophie nearly drops everything. She puts them down as calmly as she can.

"Hello Sophie," Mr Quah says.

"I was hoping to see you," Sophie replies.

Part of her wishes she could hug him but that might be inappropriate.

She asks, "How did you go? You made the trip back safely."

Mr Quah nods and says, "Only just. Let's not worry about that. We're going to stop Miss Serizawa, Sophie. Look here . . . ."

Mr Quah is excited and turns to walk.

Sophie has noticed Mr Quah's appearance before. But now that she knows him a bit better there is something else she has noticed. Mr Quah never seems stressed. He never frowns, nor panics, nor acts angry. Surely things bother him yet he always acts as if everything is going to work out. He must feel that good things happen and bad things happen so he doesn't ever worry about minor details.

Sophie believes there is another side to him. Something is very mysterious about this Mr Quah.

Mr Quah leads Sophie to the lounge. He places the locked briefcase on the coffee table. Mr Quah is not letting the case get out of his sight.

"I have one rib bone locked here," Mr Quah explains, "and this morning I waited out the front of a bank in the city. The second rib bone is now in a bank vault under an alias with a note in case you and I are unsuccessful. The note tells an old partner of mine the whole story including what we have tried, and I guess failed at, so they at least know what not to do."

Sophie says, "We are so close now aren't we."

Sophie feels more confident now that Mr Quah is back.

"One step to go and Miss Serizawa will be stopped," she says.

Mr Quah nods and says, "I hope the next step is not the hardest, but it probably will be."

He thinks back to running from the two murderous men and knocking one of them out.

Then Mr Quah finally opens the briefcase. Sophie peers inside. A frail old bone lies on a pillowcase.

"The bone looks so ordinary. I thought this would be glowing or something," she says.

Apart from fake smiles to her friends, Sophie has not appeared very happy for quite some time. She feels relieved that the bone is right in front of her, but fear remains in the forefront of her mind as their plan is not over yet. One final challenge remains.

"We need to make sure this works," Sophie states. "We should find out how to crush the bones and somehow administer them to Miss Serizawa. Eating the fragments will be the best way so the properties are absorbed into the body."

"When are we ever going to get Miss Serizawa to eat something we make? She will be suspicious," Mr Quah points out.

"I could go back to that little bookstore," Sophie suggests, "and see if they have any information on foods or poisons. There might be cases in medical journals where people have been poisoned."

"That sounds good but you have to be careful. I might go to the library in the city. We'll meet up in the afternoon."

"Excellent," Sophie says and stands to leave.

Mr Quah shows her out to the waiting Mr Nguyen.

An hour later, Mr Quah rings Sophie's boss. He books Sophie to clean his apartment again that afternoon, a different apartment of course.

"I've heard you have a good cleaner there, called Sophie," he says.

Mr Quah laughs to himself as he tries to come up with yet another false name.

The witnesses to last night's boat crash wake up feeling very ordinary. Although they know sake will apparently leave the consumer virtually hang-over free, depending on quality and quantity, they also know not to believe everything they read. Lack of sleep may contribute to the feelings of queasiness currently being experienced. But the alcohol poisoning, or sleep deprivation, or a combination of both, has amounted in a case of short-term memory loss. For it is not until much later in the day, when the two lovebirds venture out on daily errands, do they see a salvage team operating on some horrible mess of metal and fibreglass and other modern and expensive building materials out on the water. This rings a bell to both.

"The speedboat and the expensive looking yacht," the young man says.

Hand in hand the two walk to their local produce market. Upon conversing with the well informed staff, who hear gossip from far and wide, the couple learn that the speedboat operator was not to be found and that, "the yacht is owned by that group who has offered millions of dollars to those women that go around killing people."

Near midday Sophie travels by tram and then walks to the little bookstore down Origin Alley. She knows the way off by heart now. Once inside, she heads straight for books about food and cooking. She wonders if the shop assistant recognises her. Sophie wants to see if any books mention bone. Almost instantly she finds soups and stews which use bones for flavour but they are obviously fresh meaty bones. Not thousand year old brittle bones.

Sophie struggles to find anything else, but she does come up with a few ideas.

'Jelly is made from pig's feet. Well it was if it isn't anymore. But I doubt Miss Serizawa will eat some jelly I bring around to her.'

Sophie walks out of the bookstore. She is troubled. All she can come up with is crushing the bones and adding the powder to something completely different and getting the mix inside Miss Serizawa but she can't think beyond that. She can't fill in the gaps which frustrates her.

Sophie catches the tram back towards her home.

One message is on her home answering machine from Mr Nguyen.

"There is apartment to clean this afternoon. I pick you up three o'clock," the loud voice tells her.

Sophie hopes the client is Mr Quah. Sophie hopes he has had more luck than her.

Chapter Eighteen

Later in the afternoon Mr Quah opens this apartment door for Sophie, to her great relief.

They sit in the lounge room and get right to talking. Mr Quah is excited but lets Sophie go first.

"All I found is soup and stew meals. I didn't find anything helpful, but I thought that we can crush the bones, like jelly is made, and we add the powder to something. But we already knew this."

Sophie feels bad that she hasn't come up with very much.

"I thought about that at the library and read a passage about the blue lotus flower which was used in ancient Egypt. People who had this would experience a state of wellbeing. They would have the flower at parties and dance around all night. I then went and searched for more information about the blue lotus flower only to find the genetic components are basically the same as gingko biloba. I'm thinking we add our crushed bones to gingko biloba in the hope that this will increase the Phoenix blood's potency and speed up the process."

"Let's do it," Sophie says, ready to try this. "Now we need to work out how to get the concoction into Miss Serizawa's blood stream. Did you find out a way we could do this?"

Mr Quah happily says, "I found out two very interesting pieces of information while I was reading through poison books and medical journals. I even read information about poisonous darts."

"Sounds exciting," Sophie says.

Mr Quah winks and continues, "There was an article about a man who was stabbed and bled to death and all that was found near him was a puddle of water."

"I've heard about this myth," Sophie says.

"This is no myth," Mr Quah says. "He was stabbed with an icicle which pierced his heart and then melted away. No finger prints, no murder weapon."

Mr Quah feels as if this could be possible and is willing to make up an icicle of their own to try. Sophie is not so sure.

"So we grind the bone, add gingko biloba and water to the bone powder, and pour the liquid into a mould to freeze. I do like the sound of this, but how do we keep the icicle frozen? I can't have melting ice sitting in my pocket dripping through my jacket. I can see that people might be killed by huge icicles falling on them but actually being stabbed with one would be rare. And difficult for us," Sophie says.

"Sorry. I guess the idea is foolish," Mr Quah admits. "There will be a wound from the stabbing which will look like murder anyway, regardless whether forensics find a murder weapon or not. And then it's only a matter of time before the police interview all of Miss Serizawa's associates."

"The idea is great," Sophie says. "I'd love to try to make an icicle."

Sophie tries to encourage Mr Quah for his ideas. In their situation they need to stay open minded.

He studies his shoes for a minute and then raises his eyes back up.

"I've had a thought. Why does the weapon have to be ice? Obviously ice would be great but we are all going to be there to hide evidence and cover the murder up."

Sophie is interested.

"What are you thinking?" she asks.

"Bone," Mr Quah says with a twinkle in his eyes. "Instead of crushing the whole thing I'll shape the end of part of the rib making this sharp enough to be a weapon. One of us stabs Miss Serizawa. Miss Serizawa dies. We hide the evidence."

Sophie likes the idea. This has less risk of failing. There is more of a risk of going to jail for life though.

"Have a look what I've bought," Mr Quah says, carefully changing the topic.

He shows her a new pestle and mortar and a bottle of gingko biloba tablets.

Mr Quah says, "This is to crush the remaining fragments of rib into powder for whatever use we come up with."

"Can I start grinding the rib?" Sophie asks.

"First things first," Mr Quah replies.

He takes the valuable contents out from the briefcase and snaps the rib bone in half. He returns one half and puts the other half into a pillowcase. He takes the

pillowcase outside while Sophie tips the
bottle of tablets into the mortar and begins
to grind them. Sophie can see Mr Quah
outside bashing the bag with a rubber
mallet.

As the tablets turn to powder Mr Quah
comes back inside and pours the contents
of the bag into the mortar.

Sophie keeps grinding, mixing the
lumps of bones with the gingko biloba
powder.

"My arms are getting tired," Sophie
tells Mr Quah.

"I'll take over if you like," he offers.

He takes the pestle and grinds away
for a few more minutes until the bones are
all mixed in. When he stops the mortar
contains a pile of powder which looks very
innocent.

"I don't know what to say," Sophie
says with apprehension. "Things are really
moving fast now. Will this work or not?"

Sophie has to leave as the time she is
supposed to be cleaning is up. She must go
to her next client.

"We won't see each other again until
the big moment," Mr Quah tells her. "I'll

keep the powder and try to make some poisonous darts. Also, I'll take the piece of bone that is in the briefcase and shape the end to make a sharp point."

"I hope the bone is not too brittle. We need a weapon that is firm enough to stab into flesh as well as muscle and no doubt knock into other bones."

"All we can do is try," Mr Quah says.

"Good luck to you, Mr Quah."

"Stay safe, Sophie," he says.

Sophie carries her cleaning products to Mr Nguyen's waiting van.

"I'm going out to dinner with Kayami and Shing tomorrow night. Do you want to invite Rieko over and rent some movies?"

She doesn't want to tell her daughter the truth and scare her.

"That would be great!" Alana calls out from her room.

"We might be out late. Is that alright?" Sophie says.

Sophie knows in her head there are undercover police continuously parked out the front so her daughter will be safe but having her daughter home while this is the biggest night of Sophie's life is still a scary thought.

"We'll be fine, Mum," Alana assures her mum. "You worry so much."

Chapter Nineteen

Sophie realises that tonight she has a fifty percent chance of dying. She has never knowingly done anything with those odds before. As a child, falling off her bicycle one Christmas, a cut knee is the worst injury that ever happened. As a teenager, going on a roller coaster, as exciting and terrorising as the ride was, there was little chance of receiving a fatal injury. Even in the car accident Sophie had just days after she gave birth to Alana, Sophie only incurred minor injuries. There has never been a situation in her life that Sophie knows may end in her death. Tonight Sophie is walking towards an event that she may not live to talk about. Despite this she is more determined than ever.

Standing in Kayami's lounge is Miss Serizawa, Azuna, Fusako, Kayami and Sophie, the entire gang, all unrecognisable with the five of them sporting the Maiko make-up and matching styled hair.

The whole city is scared senseless of these five women. The entire country is on edge and wants these women stopped but the authorities have no idea who the women are or when they will strike next.

Here we all are, Sophie thinks to herself.

People around the world have latched on to this news story and are waiting eagerly to hear that these women have been captured and the nightmare is over.

This will end soon, Sophie keeps telling herself.

The colours in the room are hypnotic. Sophie is actually impressed by the matching oriental outfits they are wearing. The clothes are predominately white silk but are decorated with gold, red and black little designs. The tops they are wearing are flowing but hold to the body in parts. Weapons can easily be hidden under their tops. The pants they have on allow the wearer to run and jump easily.

This is the first time Sophie has seen them all together like this.

Sophie remembers why they are there and instantly stops enjoying the ambience.

Only moments earlier Sophie was outside.

Such a peaceful night, Sophie had thought to herself.

The light fog was relaxing. Sophie loves fog. In the alleyway she suddenly sees a white shadowy figure. Newspapers and television newsreaders have been telling the public to stay indoors at night. They have been warning people to hide from any pale shadowy figure. Sophie walks right up to this one. It's Azuna. Without a sound Azuna motions Sophie inside. Sophie herself is a pale shadowy figure and feels very out of place. She is one that the population has been warned about. She can't believe what she is involved with.

Inside, Sophie sees Fusako and Kayami and she wonders how Kayami is feeling. Not long later Azuna comes in from the fog with Miss Serizawa.

They have all been running around in the dark like ninjas but due to their quiet lurkings the four pale figures have all managed to sneak inside to be with Kayami without being seen once. Sophie feels claustrophobic. Relaxed on the couch cuddling a loved one, this room would appear quite large but five women standing around about to murder a man is different.

Kayami's husband is apparently sleeping down the hall.

Kayami leads the way. The other four follow silently.

Mr Quah lays very awake with a little torch on under the blanket ready for the ambush. When the quilt comes off his eyes will already be adjusted to the light.

Mr Quah hears a click and waits for what seems like forever but five people need to enter the room so he counts to ten in an attempt to slow his heart rate.

A lot can happen within a few seconds:

Mr Quah throws off the quilt and shoots a poisonous dart at the first person he sees—Fusako. The dart strikes her left cheekbone. Fusako and the dart fall to the floor. Mr Quah throws the sharpened bone to Sophie who turns and attempts to slash Miss Serizawa. Mr Quah shoots a dart at Azuna which misses. Kayami backs out of the room quietly. Azuna runs for the door to chase Kayami. Mr Quah lines her up and shoots another dart. This sticks into Azuna's right arm and she collapses. Mr Quah sees Sophie struggling with Miss Serizawa. Miss Serizawa has knocked the bone out of Sophie's hand. Mr Quah gets up and as he moves shoots a dart at Fusako which penetrates her neck while she tries to stand. He then attempts to pounce on Miss Serizawa. She is ready for the attack though and avoids him. At the same time Miss Serizawa kicks Sophie's legs out from under her. Sophie falls down. As Mr Quah comes back at Miss Serizawa she throws something at his face. Mr Quah is blinded and turns away to wipe his face with his arm. Miss Serizawa now pulls an old sickle from her robes.

"You think I wasn't ready for this! I've known your plan this whole time. I've seen you following me, you ignorant man. I've had people following you and Sophie for weeks. I ordered them to kill you in China but they failed so I'm going to finish you right now!"

Kayami runs in with a kitchen knife and stabs Miss Serizawa through her shoulder blades, which is enough for Miss Serizawa to release her grip on the sickle. This gives Sophie a chance. She shoves the brittle old bone as hard as she can into the same wound. Miss Serizawa runs around the room screaming. Sophie, Mr Quah and Kayami watch, scared, but before long Miss Serizawa crumbles and turns into a pile of dust.

Azuna and Fusako are lying on the floor passed out. Mr Quah checks Azuna's pulse.

"She'll live," he says.

He couldn't care less. The most important thing to him is Miss Serizawa is dead.

"What just happened?" Kayami asks, looking very pale.

"All the years must have caught up to her," Sophie says to Mr Quah.

"And she hasn't finished her 'task'. I hope she floats around in limbo for the next billion years," Mr Quah replies.

"Did I kill her?" Kayami asks.

She sits down on the floor. She thought her husband was going to die tonight. She has no idea what has happened.

"You just saved your husband's life," Sophie says to Kayami and puts a hand on her shaking shoulder.

"He is safe with the police. What did Miss Serizawa throw at me?" Mr Quah asks.

"She threw what's known as a Metsubushi—an eggshell filled with anything like ash, ground-up pepper, flour or dirt and sometimes gunpowder and fragments of glass. Just a way to temporarily blind you," Kayami explains.

"She succeeded."

"Is there any chance Miss Serizawa could find her way back to Earth or whatever planets exist in a billion years?" Sophie asks Mr Quah.

"I don't think the Gods will allow that. Let's not worry about her," Mr Quah says.

As far as Mr Quah is concerned the ordeal is over.

"Oh, I'm not worried. I'm very happy," Sophie is completely calm. "Let's get rid of the ashes."

Sophie notices Kayami is in a state of shock. Kayami seems to be in a waking dream. Her eyes are open but glazed over.

"Come on, let's clean this up," she says in an attempt to take Kayami's mind off recent events.

Sophie takes Kayami to find a dustpan and broom while Mr Quah builds a fire in the lounge fireplace.

When Sophie comes back she asks, "Should we separate the ashes? You know, so they can't reform."

"Why not?" Mr Quah says with a smile.

Kayami has swept up the ashes of Miss Serizawa and Mr Quah puts half in the fire. The three watch the ash burn away.

"I'll tip the rest into the river on my way home," Mr Quah says.

"What do we do with those two?" Kayami asks and points down the hall to the bedroom where Azuna and Fusako remain.

"They will wake soon enough," Mr Quah says.

One morning the old man from Yue Shan receives a knock at his door.

"Hello?" the old man calls out.

There is a shuffling of feet and an old man answers the door to see a postman standing there.

"I am here to deliver this," the postman says.

The old man takes the package from the postman.

"Thank you," the old man says.

He is about to ask if the postman needs a drink but the postman walks off down the mountain path.

Inside his hut the old man sits down and opens the package. Having anything sent to him is very rare. He can't actually remember the last time something came to him in the mail since the valley was flooded.

In the package is a note which says:

'You may be able to use this. I know you are serving your punishment but the bone worked for us. Thank you for everything.'

Sophie has signed the letter at the bottom.

The old man picks up the bone that Mr Quah earlier retrieved from the bank vault.

If the bone works he will be able to die now whenever he decides to.

After the event in Kayami's apartment Miss Serizawa's restaurant has been closed. A sign on the door reads:

'Closed for personal reasons.'

Miss Serizawa didn't have a will or any relatives. Her body is never to be found by police. Despite an investigation, which includes interviewing everyone she knew, no one is able to share any information to help the police. No foul play is recorded and because no body has been found the police eventually name Miss Serizawa as a missing person.

Azuna, Fusako and Kayami are still recovering mentally from the whole ordeal but weeks later they decide to buy Miss Serizawa's business for a small fee. This is agreed to by lawyers involved and the money from the sale is cheerfully donated to charities. They never mention Miss Serizawa again.

Initially the media has a field day over the fact that a much-loved local icon has mysteriously disappeared. Stories of how nice a lady Miss Serizawa was come from far and wide. Tributes pour in from patrons, friends and rivals. Some reporters, and members of the general public, have vague suspicions that upon Miss Serizawa's disappearance the activities of The Four Little Maids seem to have come to an apparent end. They keep their feelings to themselves, however, fearing that these thoughts may be incorrect and the nightmare that has festered over the past few weeks could flare up once more.

Azuna, Fusako and Kayami will reopen the restaurant after the shocked population has had time to divulge all of the stories.

Sophie does not want anything to do with the restaurant. In fact she hasn't spoken to any of the three women since the night in Kayami's apartment. She and her daughter want to be left alone for a while.

Mr Quah decides to use the holiday leave he has been saving up.

Mr Quah will be back in
'Timeless'